To Grandma,
Love Amelia xx
Amelia

SPINE – CHILLERS

NORTH & EAST YORKSHIRE
Edited by Sonia Gill

First published in Great Britain in 2016 by:

 Young**Writers**

Remus House
Coltsfoot Drive
Peterborough
PE2 9BF
Telephone: 01733 890066
Website: www.youngwriters.co.uk
All Rights Reserved
Book Design by Ashley Janson
© Copyright Contributors 2016
SB ISBN 978-1-78624-172-6

Printed and bound in the UK by BookPrintingUK
Website: www.bookprintinguk.com

FOREWORD

Enter, Reader, if you dare...

For as long as there have been stories there have been ghost stories. Writers have been trying scare their readers for centuries using just the power of their imagination. For Young Writers' latest competition Spine-Chillers we asked students to come up with their own spooky tales, but with the tricky twist of using just 100 words!

They rose to the challenge magnificently and this resulting collection of haunting tales will certainly give you the creeps! From friendly ghosts and Halloween adventures to the gruesome and macabre, the young writers in this anthology showcase their creative writing talents.

Here at Young Writers our aim is to encourage creativity and to inspire a love of the written word, so it's great to get such an amazing response, with some absolutely fantastic stories. We will now choose the top 5 authors across the competition, who will each win a Kindle Fire.

I'd like to congratulate all the young authors in *Spine-Chillers - North & East Yorkshire* - I hope this inspires them to continue with their creative writing. And who knows, maybe we'll be seeing their names alongside Stephen King on the best seller lists in the future...

Jenni Bannister

Editorial Manager

CONTENTS

Sacred Heart RC School, Redcar

Scarborough Pupil Referral Unit, Scarborough

Sirius Academy West, Hull

South Hunsley School & Sixth Form College, North Ferriby

Upper Wharfedale School, Skipton

Wilberforce College, Hull

THE MINI SAGAS

The Deep

Dark as coal, cold like the winter in Antarctica. Black. The fog was rapidly creeping in around the boat, and *bang*. Echoes around the ship screaming, 'Save me, help me! Join me!' There were wooden planks creaking around and snapped in half a body was floating on the surface crying for help. The weather changed and the storm came around like a volcano erupting. The boat had disappeared and all that was remaining was a man sat there fighting for his life and he had gone. His hand risen and his blood was surrounding, but how did he die dramatically?

Kyle Douglass (15)

The Shadow In The Attic

Lightning struck the side of the debilitated house. Midnight! Storms rose from the dead and grew colder by the second. The wind whistled as it brushed across the young girl's face. She entered. Cobwebs dangled from the contaminated ceilings. Fragments of dust led to an enfeebled attic. Darkness fell in front of her. She crept towards the room, but the door slammed shut, leaving her locked inside. She found a switch which was dim, but it gave some light. Unnoticed, a shadow appeared from behind the young girl. She screamed as the shadow leapt towards her...

Beth Constantine (15)

Hunted

Blood trickled down my sore wrists, where the rope once was. I peered into the darkness, the dim moonlight poured through the small bared window, highlighting the skeletons. Slowly, I tiptoed my way through the dark room. *Drip, drop.* I froze! *Drip, drop.* There it was again. A cold draught chilling me to the bone. I continued to weave a way through the corpses whilst fog pooled at my feet. *Slam!*
Heavy footsteps got louder and louder. Closer and closer. I couldn't bring myself to move. His breath warmed the air. I dropped to my knees.
Bang.

Ellie Foster (13)

All Gone

My breath feeling sharper than ever before, each breath I inhaled causing a harsh stab in my throat. My bag heavy, holding weapons and survival equipment. Tears streaming down my cheeks remembering the loss of my companions. Running against time as the groaning gradually became louder, as they crept near. 'Brains!' they called out. 'Brains!' Machete by my side drenched in the blood of my best friend. Fog slowly stopping my vision, I could see the innocent town that once was safe, behind me. Bloodthirsty people mistaking humans for zombies roaming around. It's clear that all safety had disappeared.

Sarah Tunstall (12)
Barlby High School, Selby

The Playground Of Horrors

Nightmares. They are not just our imagination playing with our minds: they are the horrible and dreadful memories of our past coming to haunt us. I can remember the ominous and blood-curdling howls sweeping across the floorboards of the corridor. The insidious screams and sinister cackles still invade and corrupt my tender mind. Trees with long, twisted branches that look like hands coming down to grab you as you stand helpless. And the feeling of being exposed to the brightness of the full, beaming moon: like thousands of piercing eyes. This is where evil comes out to play. Goodnight...

Siân Ayre (13)
Bedale High School, Bedale

Frozen

The loft was dusty, filled with decorations and toys. I finally found the tree box. Suddenly, I spotted a metal tin. Inside was old photos and old war medals. I picked them up and heard my mother shout. Throwing it back, I got out. Minutes later, I heard heavy footsteps up there. I must have been hearing things.
As I went to bed, I passed the loft and heard shouting. I felt worried as I climbed into bed.
That night, I woke up to see a dark figure hovering above my face. I couldn't move my body at all. Frozen!

Dean Paling (15)
Education Other Than At School, Middlesbrough

Weekend Away From Hell

We arrived at Centre Parcs. We unpacked and put the kettle on. The phone rang, a strange voice said about a problem with the zip wire we'd booked for the next morning. We were told not to worry, it had been fixed.

Although worried, we succeeded to take the challenge. As the rest of the family zoomed down, it was now my turn. I fastened my harness and jumped. Suddenly the wire snapped; I tumbled to the ground. Hanging from the wire, I met my death. My soul seeking revenge on my murderer.

I will find out who killed me!

Courtney Moore (15)
Education Other Than At School, Middlesbrough

The Loft

She climbed into the loft and turned on the light. Silvery webs stretched across the room and a shiver went down her spine. The kids shouted, 'Come on Mammy get the tree down.' She knew she had to get it down.

She closed her eyes and gulped. She grabbed the first dusty box, it was closed. She slowly opened it to see what was in. A webby, mushy mass with tiny little spiders crawling about stopped and looked at me. She let out a loud cry and her foot got stuck in the ladder. *Bang!* She fell to the floor...

Chantelle Hodgson (15)
Education Other Than At School, Middlesbrough

The Taunting

3:15, John lay in bed asleep. *Knock, knock, knock.* Confused, he opened his eyes and threw on his dressing gown, running down the stairs he unlocked the door; his porch was empty.

Returning to his room, a message in blood glistened in the light. Saying, 'You're next.' He darted down the stairs. *Click.* The door locked. He ran to the back door and it was already open. Suddenly it slammed shut, the Devil was taunting him.

John started sweating, his heart pounded like a drum, a noise, he turned, *smack*, darkness surrounded him. John was no more. He lay silent.

Ethan Rudd (15)
Education Other Than At School, Middlesbrough

The Ghost

I was alone in the classroom waiting for some more students to join me. Out of the corner of my eye, I saw a green figure. I turned my head and it had gone. Shivers made my hairs stand up. The air chilled. I felt scared so I tried to get out the classroom, but the door was locked. I heard footsteps and the furniture started to lift and move. I began to kick the door to alert people where I was. Suddenly, I felt a gripping sensation around my throat. My life flashed before my eyes. The door opened...

Josh Kelly (15)
Education Other Than At School, Middlesbrough

Beauty In One's Last Breath

Death. Such a crude word. So abrupt. It takes out all the beauty; the fear and the pain. Each sensual moment is to be pleasured, not quick and unpleasant. The freshly sterile blade brushed against the velvet cloth The paralysed victim's eyes widened. His sore lips released a screeching echo. The sharp point pierced his tender flesh. The victim sensed what was inevitable. A small tear sloped down his colourless neck. The blade pushed further. Blood gushed like a waterfall. Each millimetre a new picture. So beautiful. His disobedient hands weakened. But the first stoke had only just been painted...

Daanish Sohail Sonawala (14)

Hymers College, Hull

The Old Red Brick House

Recently I rented an old red-brick house. When I first moved in I felt a cold breeze running past me in the middle staircase as I headed to the kitchen. The stained-glass Victorian shade swung violently and I heard angry voices echoing upstairs. I heard banging in the kitchen, the cupboard was opening, I didn't know what to do. I left my home upstairs, I was on the step, I didn't want to go upstairs. I ran outside, no one was there. I heard the front door slam behind me. I ran and ran for help!

Chloe Green

Mowbray School, Bedale

The Abandoned House

On a very hot night, the wind, which was very strong, blew the roof of the abandoned house. I held onto the pipes on the wall so I wouldn't blow away.

It was completely dark, you couldn't even see the moon.

I knew I'd got to run away before the house fell down. I heard a Herculean wind and I started running from the house before it collapsed.

The light was dimming and I knew I had to get to safety.

As I ran from the house I could hear the house splinter and crack as it fell down.

Thomas James Scott (15)

Mowbray School, Bedale

The Dark Woods

I could sense evil in the air as I was walking in the dark woods. It went really cold, someone was watching me. I turned around and no one was there. I knew it was not a dream, so I walked deeper into the woods. The clouds got really dark and the moon went behind the clouds. Suddenly, it went pitch-black. The leaves were dry when I walked on them. I could hear the leaves rustle and the sound of footsteps following me. My heart was beating fast, I did not know what to do.

Bryony Levitt

Mowbray School, Bedale

The Abandoned House

This story is about an abandoned house and a forest.
I went to my nana's, I had to walk past the abandoned house. The old abandoned house stood on the edge of town in a snowy, freezing night in January.
Chloe walked past the abandoned house to visit me. We went to the church and when we looked in, we thought we saw a dark figure. When Chloe went into the church the dark figure had vanished. I felt really scared because the dark figure had vanished. I know it was a ghost.

Cassidy Matthews

Mowbray School, Bedale

Black Abandoned House

I went to the black ugly abandoned house. Whoever went into the house did not come out of it again.
One day, someone went in the abandoned house. That person was my friend Tom. I felt angry then I went into the house to look for him: I was really worried in case he never came out, people had told me that the abandoned house was haunted. The moon was shining through the trees. I saw Tom through the broken window, he was lying on the floor. I went into the house, by the time I got there, he'd vanished.

Ryan Richards (14)

Mowbray School, Bedale

Alvin And The Haunted Tablet

A small brown and peach-coloured rabbit named Alvin was walking through the dark, foggy woods, wearing a red-hooded jumper. He walked to Bedale Park carrying a black rucksack and a torch. Alvin was trying to figure out a code on a golden tablet, when someone tried to take it from him. Even when he turned his torch on he could not see them but he would not give up, so he pulled on the tablet to try and get it back. He got the tablet back but now they had taken his rucksack. Alvin chased them to church.

Cora Jeff

Mowbray School, Bedale

The Hidden Church

The church was hidden by dusk. The caretaker, who was lighting candles and praying for his wife who had died last week in a frightening car accident, was shocked when the power went out. The silence spread through the church. In the distance he heard a car engine and police siren.The police arrived almost right away and ran with great speed past the pews, through the cloakroom and outside to the cemetery. They were searching for the stranger who had left his footprint just outside the bank which matched the footprint beside the car door of the caretaker's wife.

William Hall

Mowbray School, Bedale

The Shadow

On a wretched stormy night, when the thunder growled above, I walked into a deep, dark forest and then I got lost. I kept hearing things in this forest like howling animals. They sounded like they were right behind me. The scream got louder but when I looked behind me there was nothing. I kept looking around to see where the sound was coming from and glimpsed a movement from behind a tree. I could see the shadow of a large, unfamiliar animal; big red eyes looked at me. I tried to run, but it was too late...

Heidi Marsden

Mowbray School, Bedale

The Short Cut

On a cold, wet night, I came back from a party and I took a short cut through the forest, I got lost. It was a nightmare. I could hear a disturbing howl. It was coming from behind the tall hedge. The howl did not seem to be from this world. I could just about see a shadow creeping towards me. I started to run, stumbling over some slippery rocks. My new shoes and my new dress were covered in mud and blood from my cut leg. The howling shadow came closer and closer. I sensed evil in the air...

Tori Scholes

Mowbray School, Bedale

The Intruder

The lightning struck the church in the late evening and it caused a big hole in the roof. The vicar, James Smith, was just heading to a church fund-raising meeting. On his way out, the bricks, tiles and concrete collapsed on him and he was buried under the wreckage. A gap near his face helped him to breathe. Eventually, he heard the handle of the church door screeched open as the intruder slowly stepped towards him and he felt a wave of hope but the footsteps slowly disappeared and his desperation grew.

Harvey Stockdale

Mowbray School, Bedale

The Cold Forest

I was walking in a forest, it was cold, I pulled up my coat, it started to rain. The forest was pitch-black, the trees were bare, brown leaves were all over the slippery ground. The sky was grey and black, you couldn't see the stars or the moon. Behind me I could hear footsteps as they splashed in puddles. I turned around quickly and saw a large man carrying a big round log. I ran, grabbing hold of branches to stop myself falling over. I stopped briefly to check that he wasn't still following me. I didn't see anyone.

Liam Evans

Mowbray School, Bedale

Something In The Church

I was supposed to meet Jack around midnight after his shift at the pub. I walked to the church, it was foggy, dark and cold. I tried to open the big wooden door by turning the metal handle. I went inside, perhaps Jack was already there. In the corner of my eye, I glimpsed a shadow. I walked carefully after it, it moved to the front of the church quickly. I hid behind a pillar. The fog started to enter the church covering the floor and pews. I felt hot breath on my neck. A cold hand touched my shoulder.

Elspeth Wright

Mowbray School, Bedale

The Mysterious Man

It was a stormy night, the rain lashed onto me. I saw an abandoned house beside a lake. It was difficult to see in the rain but I thought I saw a person beside the lake. He was suspicious.
Then the man left his bag by the lake. I waited for him to leave and I looked in the bag. It was full of fish he was illegally catching.
I hid in a tree to watch the man catching fish, but when he came back ten other men were with him and they were selling fish to other people.

Christoper Gordon Gunn (16)

Mowbray School, Bedale

The Shadow

At midnight, I went to the church, I saw a light, it was actually a fireplace. I sat by it, feeling lonely and cold. Outside the wind was calling me. I felt like there was no hope out there. I heard banging on top of the bell tower as something clanged. I went to check it out. I tiptoed slowly up the stairs. I saw a dark human-shaped shadow near the bell. It looked up and saw me coming. It disappeared. I ran to where it stood, I could smell blood where the shadow had been. Outside, I heard thunder.

Phillip Sorbie

Mowbray School, Bedale

The Last Of Us

On a freezing cold, raining night, I was lost from my group in a dark forest on an island. I was desperate to see light. All I could see was the full moon. Suddenly, I heard a strange noise in some trees. It sounded like a wolf howling. I moved towards the noise with just a knife which I found in a dusty cave on the floor. I hit the tree, but there was no response. So I slowly backed away from the tree. I thought I was the last survivor of the survival games. But I was wrong!

Morando Westfield (16)

Mowbray School, Bedale

The Knock At The Door

One stormy night, Lizzie, Maddie and Kitty sat staring at the clock waiting for the dead to arrive. Every 100 years, the dead come back to life. It was as if the whole world was at a standstill. Nothing budged, not even a drop of rain. Suddenly, there was a knock at the door, a sharp knock. Trembling, Lizzie opened the door. A bloodsucking vampire stood with his fangs out, ready to suck the sisters' blood... One by one, the sisters dropped dead in a blink of an eye. Till this day the sisters roam around Ever After High...

Aminah Hussain (12)
Outwood Academy, Middlesbrough

The Stairs

There's a light at the top of the stairs. Its harsh glow promises sanctuary. The stairs creak as I step on them. In desperation, I freeze, I listen to any sounds of movement. Relieved, I hear nothing. Carefully, I take another step. I freeze again as the steps creak, not daring not to look at anything other than beckoning radiance. A third step, louder this time, I don't stop, I run up the stairs. I race towards the light. My feet thunderous against the dark. The sudden hand against my ankle. I fall! Suddenly, I'm up the stairs. I'm relieved.

Kieron Kevin Wilson (13)
Outwood Academy, Middlesbrough

Strangers

There I stood, about 20 steps from a rotted, abandoned, haunted house. Finally reaching the door, I looked up and stared at the stained glass. My heart was racing with fear. I didn't know if it was what I thought it was. My hand reached out for the rusty doorknob and the door opened with a creak. A shadow flew across the room. 'Hello? Anyone there?' No reply. Suddenly, a wicked scream thundered around the room. I approached a mirror but my reflection was not looking back...

Chelsea Chantal Fernand Tate (12)

Outwood Academy, Middlesbrough

To Be Hunted Down

He could hear them crawling up the stairs towards him. They were so close, he could hear their heavy breath. His heart beat faster and harder like a train at full speed. He could smell the sweat of the blood-hungry monsters. He stared at the door trying to decide if he could face the terror. He could smell the garlic of his family from downstairs. As he opened his eyes, he could see the door handle twisting. He cried out, 'I'll miss you my sweetheart, I've let you down. I'll never go hunting again, on my daughter's life. Promise.'

Sky-Ann Thompson (14)

Outwood Academy, Middlesbrough

Thrill To Death

As we were walking along on the road, I saw something crossing in front of me, but the rest didn't see it. We kept walking and hearing those ghostly noises, calling one of my friend's names. 'Ella!' It was that monster who was calling out the names. Then afterward, when all the street lights were off, the mysterious monster came in front of us. We were terrified and fell over. It had a spooky face and the rest of its body was invisible. It had the blood all over it! And it had two fangs in its mouth.
'Oh my... '

Patricia Bouwe Lisasaya Yambuya (12)
Outwood Academy, Middlesbrough

Phantom

Katie was the only one left on stage in front of the audience. The silhouette of the phantom lurked, wanting her to scream. 'You will now pay the consequences!' the mysterious phantom called. 'What?' Katie screamed. Her body was tied to the oak chair that creaked with every move she made. Then came the scream that pierced through the building... Then came the silence! Not a bone in her body moved, but a shiver ran down the audience. The outline of a girl floated through the air. Katie, the whole cast and teachers were nowhere to be seen...

Lauren Katie Simpson (12)
Outwood Academy, Middlesbrough

Curiosity Killed The Cat

Mommy told me to never go in the basement, but I wanted to see what was making that noise. It sounded like a puppy, so I opened the basement door and tiptoed down a bit. I didn't see a puppy. Then Mommy yanked me out of the basement and yelled at me and it made me sad, so I cried. Mommy said, 'Never go in there again!' She gave me a cookie which made me feel better, so I didn't ask her why the boy in the basement was making puppy noises, and why he had no hands or feet.

Cristian Watson (14)
Outwood Academy, Middlesbrough

The Boy Who Got Lost In The Woods While Getting Chased By A Beast

On a cold, misty night, Leo and his friend Charlie were watching 'The Walking Dead'. Leo went to get Charlie a drink, when they heard something hit the window. Leo looked suspiciously outside. It was a stone, saying, 'Watch out tonight'.
The next night, they crept into the dark woods to find whoever did this. They perched on a log in the middle of the woods. Suddenly, something sinister appeared from behind the bushes... it was a werewolf!
'Run!'
As the werewolf tore into Charlie's flesh, Leo shouted, 'Nooo! Charlie's dead forever!'

Bradley Moore (15)
Outwood Academy, Middlesbrough

Deadly Clown

Everyone squashed together in bed to watch 'Deadly Clown'. *Bang!*
'W-w-what was that?' Toby asked nervously in the middle of the movie.
'It wasn't anything. Stop being a wimp!' exclaimed Ryan.
Suddenly, the door creaked open and a silhouette of a frightening
clown stood there.
'Mum, is that you?' enquired Toby.
'No, I'm someone you've seen but not yet met! He, he, he!'
'W-w-who are you?' stammered Toby, petrified and confused.
'I am Peek-A-Boo! Your scariest movie character come alive! He, he,
he! Ha, ha, ha!' he laughed maniacally. 'Let's play a game kids, this
one's called *Kill! Kill! Kill!*'

Hiba Rafique (12)
Outwood Academy, Middlesbrough

Spine-Chiller

Satanic. Devilish. Diabolical. You could even say it was spine-chilling.
A demonic glow possessed it. That vile, supernatural creature was
crazed; the sight was unearthly. It was trapped under a bloodthirsty
frenzy, hissing and spitting, clawing my ankles. My face was terror-
stricken, my fingers trembling with fear. It wasn't possible to even
consider the thought of being alive after this. The death train was
chugging through my mind. Getting closer, faster, deadlier. The
obnoxious monster was lunging towards me. I couldn't tell if time
slowed or sped up... I'd been bitten. I had become one of them. A
cold-blooded spine-chiller.

Caitlin Ruth Conners (12)
Outwood Academy, Middlesbrough

Why Me?

It was one evening, a man called Jeff had been walking around the park all day, so he was shattered. He was tired, so he headed home and went to get undressed. As he got his pyjamas ready, he turned around to fold them up. But as he turned around, his wardrobe fell apart. His clothes ripped and tore apart. As the wardrobe fell down he saw some words at the back of the wardrobe, and he didn't know what to think about this horrible message. It said: 'I will be ending your life... '

Jack Winn (11)
Outwood Academy, Middlesbrough

This Dream Isn't A Dream?

Leo was a brave and courageous boy. On Halloween, Leo moved into his new home in the countryside. This house was near a castle (made in the medieval era).
Leo went to bed, but he could hear something from the castle, so he went to check it out. After entering the castle, he found himself in a room with a guillotine. Out of nowhere, people appeared. A noble sat on a grand chair, also lots of posh people. A man grabbed Leo, there was silence. The people stared at Leo... He'd been executed! No wonder the house was cheap!

Hasan Afzal (11)
Outwood Academy, Middlesbrough

Haunted House

Alex was an ordinary boy. He went to school, had friends and played video games.

On Halloween, Alex moved house to the countryside. Alex didn't want to move house, he was leaving everything behind.

Alex was exploring the house when he heard screams, it was his mother and father. 'Mum, Dad!' shouted Alex. Alex sprinted up the stairs to his parent's room. The carpet was stained with blood, the wardrobe rattled violently. 'Dad, is that you?' asked Alex, warily. The boy opened the wardrobe door, never to be seen again... The house is still claiming victims, beware!

Abdullah Afzal (13)

Outwood Academy, Middlesbrough

Friend

I'm a psychiatrist. I have a few patients, but only one of them is interesting. She's eight years old and diagnosed with schizophrenia. She's young, so her parents keep her home for our meetings. She always talks about her invisible friend - Mary.

I didn't mind her talking about Mary until her last appointment. She seemed scared and kept turning around looking at something.

Her parents didn't show up on time, I asked her why.

'They will not come back. Mary said she killed them.'

I didn't believe her, but she was right. They never appeared - guess they were murdered.

Wiktoria Mikulska (14)

Rossett School, Harrogate

Timer To Death

Tick-tock. I could hear the timer on my arm going down, seeming faster and faster. Forever I'd known the day I was going to die, everyone did, thanks to the timer on the inside of our arms. Not how, not why, not what... just when. But since everyone's timer had gone into sync, the world had gone into panic. Lockdown. Meltdown. Everything was slotting into place for me now though. The strange messages I'd kept hearing in my mind. The little fiery light in the sky, getting closer, that only I seemed to notice. Life and death were becoming one.

Jasmine Alice Tyler (14)
Rossett School, Harrogate

Spine-Chiller

Midnight. A cloak of darkness engulfs my room, swallowing me into the blackness. Pushing me onto my bed, making me feel smaller and smaller. My heart races. Did I hear something? My hands, now clammy and cold, shake anxiously. I definitely heard something downstairs. My breathing quickens. 'There's nothing downstairs, go back to sleep,' I urgently tell myself. I try to close my eyes, but I can't. They dart around the room scarily, stopping to fully look at anything. I pull my duvet further over my already sticky and hot body. I don't want to move.

Isobel Ophelia Reynolds (14)
Rossett School, Harrogate

Spine-Chillers

It was Christmas Eve, the snow was fresh and crisp. Pitsborough Road is where it all began and where it ended...

People were sleeping peacefully, except for the occasional lonely drunken man wandering in the street. Alone. This was the start. The presents wrapped, we were waiting... anticipating the clock to strike 13. Legend has it, the presents opened before Christmas Day are cursed with the worst kind of evil you can imagine. It's sad really, in an hour it will all be over and the evil curse will still exist for another year...

Caitlin Cunningham (14)
Rossett School, Harrogate

Christmas Spirit

Tap. Tap. Whisper. Whisper. Stop. Through the window, give my present. Gone. Midnight again. Next house. Next present. One person per house gets my gift. I decide, live or die, who will be free? The lucky ones get freedom. Release. Escape. The unlucky ones get left behind. Stuck here for another year with no escape. Waiting, hoping for next Christmas.

As they wake I listen with pure delight for the screams. Harrowing, heartbroken wails, rising down each house as they discover they are unlucky.

Another person gone. Another year to wait.

Imogen Fisher (15)
Rossett School, Harrogate

Sentience

As the candle flickered there was one thing, just one small thing.
A thought. *I have to leave.* The essence of a life drifted up in wisps
of smoke. He tried to move. Nothing. Silence filled the air. He was
a prisoner in his own body. His time was running out. The smell of
his burning corpse filled the air, lighting the surroundings. He could
only focus on the pain. He tried again. Nothing. Inside his head an
agonising cry echoed. Once more he tried. Once more. There was
movement, the smallest movement. He fell, setting the house ablaze...

Jacob Turner (15)
Rossett School, Harrogate

Spine-Chillers

Tick-tock, tick-tock, the sounds spinning around in my head, then the
room fell silent. The silence lingered. A howl of wind slammed the
door to my left. The torches blew out. In the spur of the moment,
I reached into my pocket in urgent search of the matches, they
dropped. My hand slid across the floor in urgent search of them. But
the matches were placed in my hand.

Joshua Merrick (15)
Rossett School, Harrogate

The Wrinkly Hand

There was a sly, quiet knock on the door, I quickly hid under my soft bed covers. There was another knock... A tickle went down my spine. I got out of my bed and walked across the creaky floorboards, seconds before I was about to twist the doorknob, a wrinkly hand came through the letterbox. My face turned pale, the hand put itself round my throat and started to choke me...

Harry Lawrence (12)

Rossett School, Harrogate

The Fright On Christmas Eve

There once was a boy called Jack who was fast asleep. It was coming up to midnight on Christmas Eve. Just when Santa was approaching his house he got taken out by an 8ft tall clown. It was white-faced, red-eyed, he wanted to give all the kids a fright.
As he approached Jack's house, he wanted to give Jack a present he would never forget. All the noise woke Jack up. The clown was right in front of Jack's face, so he rolled out and ran as fast as his legs could carry him, but it wasn't fast enough...

Hannah Sykes (11)

Rossett School, Harrogate

Solid Black Eyes

Everything was dark. I hate it when it's dark somewhere. I yelled for my family, but no reply.

I went to the living room and I saw a girl in the corner. But I didn't know who she was, so I asked her. 'Who are you?' Then she turned around. She had solid, black eyes.

I started running. But the door was locked and I got stuck in the corner. She came for me screaming. It was so loud that I passed out. I had solid black eyes the next day on Christmas Day...

Szilard Toth (11)

Rossett School, Harrogate

The Hour Night

I awoke, light footsteps on the hallway, laughter filled the house, the wind howled. Slowly, I lifted my hand and reached for the door... *bang!* The door opened, then I felt a breeze on my neck The floor creaked, blood dripped from the ceiling, a shadow ran behind me. *Bang, bang, bang!* I turned around as fast as I could. Nothing. I turned back, a girl crying, blood falling from her eyes. 'Your turn to die!' she said. A high-pitched scream. I awoke, it was a dream.

Joel Richardson (11)

Rossett School, Harrogate

Gloomy Night

One cold, gloomy winter's evening, there was a loud thunder-like crash on the door. There was a loud howl of wind screeching its way through the corridors of the scary, desolate castle.

Jeremy peeked through a hole in the old wooden door to see who it was. An old man wearing black was standing there. He looked strangely familiar. 'What do you want?' Jeremy shouted fiercely. Before he could answer, the old door crashed inwards falling off its hinges. 'Get out of our castle!' Jeremy said angrily. Then he disappeared... He was gone... Was he a ghost?

Emma Guneyogullari (11)

Rossett School, Harrogate

Clowns Are Here

Bang. Santa fell down the stairs. Everyone ran to the top of the stairs. 'It's Santa, Dad,' said the little girl.

Father tiptoed down and said, 'No it isn't. Run!' Suddenly Father was gone. His skin was hanging over the fireplace.

She ran to the police station. 'Help, help, my dad was skinned alive!' They all turned around, they were clowns! 'Come here now girl.' She ran away...

Joshua Reuben Dale (11)

Rossett School, Harrogate

Spine-Chilling Story

The hall was dark, the street was dark, the house was dark and the girl was worried. There was a knock at the door. The doorknob started to unscrew. Finally, I heard the drop of the doorknob, what was it? I went to look down the stairs, nothing was there. Was I imagining? I went to the living room, what was that? A creepy cackle filled the room. I fell to the ground. What happened? I looked up to see if the hideous creature had anything to do with it, I looked up, he was gone...

Oliver Washbrook (12)
Rossett School, Harrogate

Possessed By A Demon?

So it all started about a week go, I was playing games as all other teenage boys do. *Bang! Bang!* went the battered door. It continuously happened and when I realised no one was going to open it, I went downstairs to see who was at the door. I slowly opened the door and peered outside. A shadow, like a flash, disappeared. A cold feeling shivered down my spine. My hand immediately shut the door as I tried to shout my dad. Nothing came out of my mouth, it was like a demon was possessing me.

Georgia Anaya Golding-Saunders (11)
Rossett School, Harrogate

The Haunted House

Ben approached the haunted house. Inside ragged dolls were scattered on the floor. There was the cackling of laughter, with Ben's feet frozen to the floor. There was a dirty swamp, a creature emerged, Ben ran in terror. He reached an abandoned graveyard, zombies emerged from the dead. Five people stood on a hill, by the bright light of the moon they turned into werewolves. Ben ran rapidly, he came to a battered door, he ran through it. The dolls were singing. Tears ran down his face, he was dead as a doornail!

Ethan Ross (11)

Rossett School, Harrogate

Spine-Chiller

'Argh!' I shrieked.
One scary, gloomy night, there I was, lying in bed on Christmas Eve. I suddenly heard a knock on the door. Who was it? I had a shiver down my spine. *Oh no,* I thought, somebody was coming to capture me. Who was it! A clown, a monster or just somebody just trying to wind me up? I had a thought it was probably just a clown. Oh no, I saw him, it was 100% a clown, he was very tall and very creepy. I suddenly screamed. 'Argh!'

Joshua Teasdale (12)

Rossett School, Harrogate

The Girl

There was a little girl-like figure sat in the corner saying, 'Die, bleed!' I only had a quick second to glance at her axe.

I went to get a knife from the drawer but she was gone, my mum walked through the door, 'Enjoy your day?'

'Err, yeah!' I said.

I went to bed to try and think but suddenly, 'Die bleed,' came from my closet. Then the girl came out, her face had a smile carved into it. She smiled at me. 'Die, bleed!' a creepy laugh filled the air...

Oliver Spice (11)

Rossett School, Harrogate

Possessed

The dark, mysterious soul of the witch. The anxious screams of the little girl who just came for Halloween. She didn't seem like human. A loud bang was penetrating her mind. The mind which was changed by a second. Possessed. She was possessed by the black, crumbled heart of the ghostly witch. Repulsive, mysterious is what you call her. She was owned by the witch. The demonic call teased her, played with her. It didn't let go. It didn't let go of her poor soul.

Where is she? Where is she now?

Aerfene Conan (13)

Rossett School, Harrogate

Untitled

I sat bolt upright. I could see a clear cylinder surrounding me - and whatever it was I was sat on. I stood up, hearing noises all around me, a door creaked open in front of me. I stepped into the room that became a corridor, an extremely long corridor. It trailed down, candles lighting as I stepped past. I saw a note, it read: 'Figure this riddle, to redeem your freedom. Tell me your answer, or I will become your dream'.

I kept walking. Another note became distinct, it read: 'What am I?'
A demonic voice exclaimed, 'Time's up... !'

Mia Taylor (13)
Rossett School, Harrogate

The Wardrobe

Tom's eyes snapped open. Gasping for air, his whole body paralysed. He managed to relax, he slowly turned his head towards the wardrobe in his room. Something didn't seem right. Shaking, he sat up, not taking his eyes off the wardrobe. As if under a spell, he crept towards it. Peering into the eerily dark wardrobe, he realised there was nothing there. He gasped in shock. There on his bed was a clown, his smile cut into his pale, bloody face. His eyes darkened out, also cut, into crosses. He stumbled towards Tom slowly...

Amy Johnson (12)
Rossett School, Harrogate

My Shadow...

'I want to show you something.'
'OK.'
We slink out of the room and slowly creep up the stairs, they moan and creak under our weight. The lights on the landing don't turn on, the darkness stalks us down the hallway until we reach my room. I turn on the light. 'Wait here.'
I go over to the curtains and pull them open. Suddenly, something streaks across the floor into the corner. Jane gasps. 'I heard people are afraid of shadows.'
'But why is mine afraid of me?'

Lorimer Pepper (12)
Rossett School, Harrogate

Spine-Chillers

I was walking home from school and this tall, gloomy figure walked in front of me. I cautiously stopped, wondering what or who it was. Running home, I heard a whisper in my ear. 'I will get you one day, I will.' I tried to forget that horrifying whisper, but I couldn't. That was all that was penetrating my mind that night. As I was trying to get to sleep, I heard it again, that whisper, 'I will get you one day, I will.' I don't remember all of what happened, but I was taken by something or someone...

Maddy Newby (13)
Rossett School, Harrogate

Nameless

A sinister smile crept up towards the black abysmal pits replacing his drooping sunken eyes. She backed against the wall as he stalked towards her like a predator advancing on its prey. The girl with no name scrambled desperately to escape his treacherous clutches. The blinding light that previously illuminated the room with a dismal glow, went out, leaving the room to be plagued by the engulfing darkness. The ominous silence was abruptly broken by a loud crash. She had lost.

Caitlin Parry (13)

Rossett School, Harrogate

The Mysterious Murderer

I remember that night, the end. Anabelle, a young, beautiful girl looked out of her window into the endless forest. Her father told her to never go in there but, knowing Anabelle, she ignored him.
It was tea, her mother shouted her but there was no reply. She checked all over the house, but she was nowhere. Then her father said she might have gone into the forest. They called the police.
As they ventured further in, they heard a drip, drip, drip. Blood was pouring from the tree, and there she lay, forever a tortured soul condemned to Hell...

Emily Baker (12)

Rossett School, Harrogate

Approaching Darkness

Ominous thundering awoke me from a peaceful slumber, that's when I saw the mysterious figure enshrouded in darkness carrying a scarlet, red-tinted scythe. His voice boomed around the room echoing off the walls. He turned in my direction and said, 'Goodbye little girl.' He sprinted towards me but passed straight through and decapitated a little girl standing behind me, spreading shards of crisp and brittle bone and drops of deep red blood.

I woke up shaking, drenched with sweat, engulfed in darkness, holding onto a crimson, red-tinted scythe while standing over my beloved sister's pale, lifeless body...

Jacob Dean (12)

Sacred Heart RC School, Redcar

The Despicable Yet Devious Dragon

Unsuspecting folk embarked upon an excursion to the Tower of London prison, where the rebellious prisoners' disintegrating bodies lay. Then they heard a deceitful tale about a devious dragon. Horrendous lightning struck three times and a foul beast appeared, chandeliers were smashed, shelves annihilated, there was mass destruction. Lightning struck. *Bang!* The dragon had gone now, oozing guts dripped down the walls. Another treacherous tale called Ghastly Ghouls. Another law-breaker's carcass was decapitated, left to rot. They emerged into a gory category of cruel and villainous, soulless, wicked bodies. The scared travellers were petrified by such a horrid tale.

Ian Peter-Dale Rye (11)

Sacred Heart RC School, Redcar

The Poltergeist Path

Emma walked carefree down the wooded, misty alley until she felt the warm breathing down the back of her youthful neck... The leaves crackled beneath her feet as she ran. Falling over her shoelace, she glanced at the black shadow on the alley wall. Shivering with fear, she turned around slowly fearing someone was watching her, but nothing was there. Her long, shiny curls ripped out of her head as she was lifted up by her throat, she couldn't scream... Falling, collapsing to the floor, facing the ground, laughter was heard as she drew her last and only dying breath...

Kimi Watson
Scarborough Pupil Referral Unit, Scarborough

The Cliff Hanger

In the dark, gloomy woods branches creaked. The wind howled like the cries of a ferocious wolf waiting for dinner.
The moon glimmered like a diamond on a girl's necklace in the night sky.
The girls camped in the woods for the night around a campfire, full of scary stories. They heard a sound. What could it be?
They panicked, their hearts beating, cold sweat running down their backs. They ran as fast as they could. The sound started to follow them through the deep, dark woods. They ended up on a cliff: the only way was to jump...

Zack Blades-Wilkinson
Scarborough Pupil Referral Unit, Scarborough

The Last Halloween

The thunder clap broke the silence as we walked down the crooked pathway. We saw the sign: *Warning Le Mansion Diablo.*
The door was mysteriously open, the first step felt like the last. The door slammed shut behind us. We stepped towards the glowing light. *Hissss...* we ran up the stairs in fear and locked ourselves in.
'We need to get out of here!'
Jake tried the window. It was locked tighter than my grandma's cupboard! We opened the door, stepped out, rushed downstairs straight for the door. But suddenly the door was locked...

Leo Jagger
Scarborough Pupil Referral Unit, Scarborough

A Man At My Grandma's House

Bang! Bang! Bang! There was a knocking at the wooden door of my creepy Grandma's house... The sky darkened as we saw the man at the broken door of my grandma's house... The man walked through the woodworm-riddled door of my mysterious grandma's house. I raced through my old grandma's house. I was frightened that I would be caught, or something even worse...
'Wake up Billy, you were just dreaming,' Grandma spoke quietly, as she woke me from the evil terrible horrors of my nightmare... It was a dream, I hoped!
Bang! Bang! Bang! My hopes shattered, was it real?

Dylan Fox (12)
Sirius Academy West, Hull

Anonymous Acres

Something outlandish was following me. I started to run as fast as I could, my feet vigorously stamping on the sodden ground in rhythm with my pounding heart. Suddenly, a monstrous gale dragged me helplessly towards what looked like, a graveyard. My mind was convinced that I was being taken into an undead universe. Still dragged by the monstrous gale, I began to scan something on the derelict ground in front of me, which looked like an abandoned grave. Abruptly, I found myself laid out on the godforsaken earth, being pulled into the underground world by rapid green growing weeds...

Kira Hayward (13)
Sirius Academy West, Hull

The Mansion On Killknock Street

Once upon a time, oh, forget that...
In the dead of night in a gloomy, dark mansion at the end of Killknock Street, is a lovely, sweet girl, fast asleep. We always thought she was sleeping. But she isn't really asleep. She's a ghost. She's the first victim. She never came out. She'll open the door - the door that is only ever seen open at midnight on Halloween! Everyone says that when kids go in they never leave! My sister Alex and I don't believe this and at midnight we are going in. Then, we'll find out the truth. Finally!

Katie Popplewell (11)
Sirius Academy West, Hull

Death Walk

A horrifying shrill scream filled the air. What monstrous thing could make that freaky sound?

I was walking home alone and I was absolutely terrified, that sound stopped me in my tracks. It was dark and gloomy and the air was icy cold and thick with fog. Has someone just been murdered. I was terrified, my heart was in my mouth choking me as I tried to run home. I got to the top of my street, someone was following me; a man with a knife, with blood on it, a werewolf, a zombie? I couldn't run.

Help me please!

Kieran Warcup (14)
Sirius Academy West, Hull

Nowhere To Run

My name is Daniel. One night, I went into the attic where I saw a box that said: 'Keep out!'. Inside it was glowing, so I had a look and there was a book, which I began to read. Then, there was a banging noise outside the door. There stood a ghost. She came towards me, warning me not to read more of the book. But it was too late. Behind me there was a murderer holding a jagged knife. I stood up, trying to escape, but there were giant insects blocking all the exits. I had nowhere to run...

Bethany Percy (11)
Sirius Academy West, Hull

House Of Horror

The damp wooden floorboards lay silently... time stood still. A sudden tread tickled my cold back. Danger signals to me everywhere. I look. 'It'll be OK!' shivered Mum holding my pale, shaky hand tightly. Eerie noises were whistling in my open ears. Suddenly, there was a creak underneath my unsteady feet. I felt Mum's tiny hand squeezing mine tighter and tighter.
'Hello?' my voice echoed creepily. Mum and me grew more and more worried as we could now hear dripping. *Drip... drop... drip... drop...*
'Hello?' I repeated feeling a little like my echo. My hand slipped away from Mother's. 'Mother... ?'

Charley Magee (11)
Sirius Academy West, Hull

The Abandoned House

As I began to walk down the creaky, wooden corridor, I realised that I wasn't alone... I had been on a walk to the park when me and my friend had a huge fall out and I stormed off without her. That's when I found the house! At the end of the road, I could see a huge house. There was a long winding path leading up to the main door. I decided to go inside. It was dark and shadowy and I wondered if it was too late to turn back. And that's when I suddenly saw the ghost... !

Grace Horton (11)
Sirius Academy West, Hull

The Endless Dream

I woke up this morning early and the day was exactly the same as the day before. After the long boring day at school, I went to bed and that's how it began... In my restless dreams I could see that I went to the bathroom and looked in the mirror. I saw Menacing Woman trying to murder me! I started to scream, but nothing came out. Suddenly, her lips started to come much closer to me. I thought she had amazing make-up on, however, then I noticed that it was dripping blood. Why won't this endless dream be over?

Martyna Sondej (11)
Sirius Academy West, Hull

The Deep Dark Shadow!

As it gets closer I run, but I feel like I'm not! I look at the walls to see if I'm moving but they're all the same. All dark, dim and horrifying wallpaper, like really who picked that hideous pattern? I can't really see anything in the gloom, it's like a maze. I feel like I'm going in circles. I can feel there's something trying to grab me, but then sometimes it does! I disappear into the darkness behind me. It feels like there's a sharp pointy axe sticking in my thin skin back. I scream, but nothing comes out...

Lucy Ann Wilson (11)
Sirius Academy West, Hull

House Of Horror

I can hear the screams echoing through the entire house. The tormented beings are running through the house in a blood-curdling manner. I am paranoid of the future, wondering if they'll catch me. I'm the only living thing in this house and I probably won't stay that way. The Grim Reaper will soon take my life. This was not the place to deliver a pizza to. My friend was once in this house, but is now dead, with Satan. The ghouls, the banshees. The end is nigh. The screams, they're near. Oh no a clown. 'Please leave clown!'
'Dieee!'

Harry Kai Thompson (11)
Sirius Academy West, Hull

The Screamers

Screams. All I hear are ear-shattering screams that are so high-pitched they're almost inaudible! The screams aren't from any earthly being I know of. I first heard them four months ago, a split second before the end. There were thousands - millions even - of screamers (that's what I call the monsters) plaguing the streets near my house - my beautiful home, oh how I miss it! And tearing every last piece of flesh from the bones of my neighbours, leaving piles and piles of dry skeletons! I fled in my mum's car... they tore it apart... thriving while we're savagely, brutally eradicated...

Olivia Madsen (12)
Sirius Academy West, Hull

Eternal

Adele walked across the grubby ground waking up the midnight sounds; the ceiling stretched across the narrow roof and the dust enclosed the secret shadows. The rooms concealed mysteries, once known which are now all but forgotten. The ample corridors brought forth rumours that exposed the deep feelings of despair and isolation, which stroke her humble heart with depression. She often wondered what lay in those pleasant corners, where the sorrow purified the ponderous mourners. She stopped. Suddenly, the atmosphere started to shiver - the mighty halls began to open, blankets of darkness embraced the infinity, where the silence eternally reigned.

Favour Oluomachi Dim (13)
Sirius Academy West, Hull

They Are Behind Me!

They're behind me. Breathing down my neck. My muscles are screaming, begging me to stop. I ignore the pain. I can hear them, they're getting closer, I have to escape. My heart is beating fast, my legs are giving in, they are behind me. I fall, unimaginable mistake. They are here, surrounding my lying body like predators surrounding prey. I am crying with fear, I don't want to die, but I can't do anything. I am just lying here, and they are closing in, I can't get up, the fear of facing them makes my body go numb.

Viktorija Borovika (13)
Sirius Academy West, Hull

The Chronicles Of Black Magic

One dark and gloomy night, a group of kids went to an abandoned haunted house. When they were at the front door, Sarah had doubts. 'I don't think this is a good idea,' she said.
'Relax,' replied Jonny, 'we'll be fine.'
'Yeah!' added Henry. 'I'll hold your hand if you want.' Henry had a huge crush on Sarah and wouldn't leave her alone.
They walked into the house anxiously. When they got in, the door slammed behind them. Sarah heard a noise, she told Jonny but he just said she had imagined it.
They carried on walking.
'Boo!'
'Aarrghh!'

Josh Abbott (11)
Sirius Academy West, Hull

Willow Tree

Across from the willow tree, in a forsaken home, it lies - lifeless. Some say it's possessed by the Devil; others dare to even imagine. A hidden soul buried deep beneath the plastic walls. A horror of unusual nightmares lurks beneath the shell of beauty. The willow tree aghast from dismay, sways recklessly. A stare (a stare is all it takes) into the maleficent eyes can torture you like flames. Regrets will haunt you, as will the ominous eyes that stare upon yours. Across from the willow tree, an unforeseeable horror rests. Until the day it wakes, it will remain untouched.

Chloë Maestre-Bridger
Sirius Academy West, Hull

The Room Of Darkness

All around, I see nothing here. But am I mistaken? The walls so bitter feel like they are closing in. Not able to see or even suspect what is in front of me. I make my first step. *Crack! What was that?* I wonder, not knowing what the sound was. Attempting to turn around, I begin to feel a shiver across me, howling like the type you hear from wolves. I can't remember which way I came in. Not knowing which way to go, I anxiously make my way through the cobwebs of horror, they stick to my face...

Bethany May Robinson-Key (12)
Sirius Academy West, Hull

Appearing Doll!

The door creaks open... the dark hall appears, rusty doors leading into cobwebby rooms. Blood splattered in every corner. Where am I? Stairs spiralling up so high, mist creeps into my sight. Then, up there, in the abandoned bathroom in the white bloodstained bath appears a doll. I scream with terror and run through the wall of mist. Just as I am about to run out of the door, I come to a halt as spiders, rats scurry across the damp floorboards! Then I finally get out of the rotted, crooked door and stumble in shock to my unsteady feet!

Katelyn Appleby (11)
Sirius Academy West, Hull

No Exit

I wandered through an overgrown, silent maze, it was like someone was watching over me - like God. I walked and walked, briskly trying to get out. It seemed there was no exit. I thought to myself, *is there a treasure chest around here or a secret handle that will get me out of here?* I stopped. I stared. I saw a shadow in the distance, so I began to go like a lightning bolt. I heard a voice in the back of my ear, he whispered, 'Come out now, there is no escape.' Blood was coursing through my pulsing veins...

Liam David John Deighton (14)

Sirius Academy West, Hull

Spine-Chiller

Do you want to hear the deathly screams coming from 249 at Sirius Academy in Hull? Because in the year 2005, Sirius Academy was Pickering High School and there was a little girl who had six rag dolls. One day, there was one particular rag doll that was creepy-looking and the head teacher thought it was too scary to show the other children, so they threw it in the dump. But a deadly dark curse was placed upon this very doll and it came alive and called itself Spine Chiller... It lives in the vent of Room 249 at Sirius.

Rebecca Cameron-Skoof & Thomas Spicer-Dawson (12)

Sirius Academy West, Hull

The Dracula Tale

As the thick fog rolled in... the dark, creepy cemetery was spookier than ever. The wind was howling, the trees were whistling against the ghostly wind. The dark house was barely visible, bats flew all over. The sign was creepy and said: *People of the world you dare enter my house I will get you.* This was in blood...

I entered the house, my name is Bill. My dad told me rumours about Dracula, who apparently lived there. I went to see. I walked into Dracula at the top of the stairs, just by looking at him I died...

Joshua Court (11)
Sirius Academy West, Hull

The Room

The anxious boy reluctantly stepped through the door. The room was old and charred. It also had a slight mist spread along the floor but parted where the footsteps appeared, getting closer to where the young boy stood. Each footstep sounded like a heartbeat and a dark shadow loomed over the whimpering boy's face. He stepped back towards the door which slammed shut, accompanied by a spine-chilling scream from the figure. Its long black hair was like hay and its eyes were fire. Its arms reached out like an octopus and the boy's tears slowly turned to blood.

George Whitaker (14)
South Hunsley School & Sixth Form College, North Ferriby

A Scare Of The Night

The door creaked open to let in the whispering souls of the night. She, who lurked in the house, was aware of the mystical surroundings. Murky, the air swallowed the house and welcomed it into their realm of horrendous horror. Dark clouds clustered over the roof and settled down with a terrible surprise. What lingered outside was the unknown but she who owned the horrific house thrived off the fear of humans who visit to stay. Ghosts are closing in, revenge is on the agenda and causing harm is what they live for. Will you survive a night of scares?

Lauren Amelia Harris (13)

South Hunsley School & Sixth Form College, North Ferriby

My Zombie Friend, Or Is He Family?

The sun was covered with black, raging clouds, with the thunder and lightning attacking people. I sprinted into the forest which had an abandoned graveyard in it. I was scared, nervous and worried to run through the seven miles of graveyard to reach my house. I had never gone through the graveyard at night.
Bang! The lightning hit a tree, and the tree was falling, falling like a lion, chasing its prey for its tea. I ran through the graveyard, the tree was falling quickly. Suddenly, it hit my leg and I saw what happened behind me...

Callum Bateman (14)

South Hunsley School & Sixth Form College, North Ferriby

Where He Went

The sun was attacked by the black clouds of fear. The trees' leaves had rotted off and the house was surrounded by a blanket of black fog. One light was turned on in the house, but who could be in there? The rest of the house was abandoned and left to rot. The house towered over everything, watching everybody's every move. The boy cautiously moved closer to the house. Of course, with his curious personality, he would want to see what was in the house. A hand grabbed his shoulder and before he knew it, he was being buried alive.

Amelia Riley (13)
South Hunsley School & Sixth Form College, North Ferriby

In The Shadows

Darkness filled the sky. The rusty wind chime swayed frantically in the wind. Black fog surrounded me. The only thing I could see through it was a house, a terrifying one too. As I crept to the door, I realised that it was already open. I walked in, looking everywhere. You know that spine-chilling feeling when you know someone is watching you? When you see something out of the corner of your eye? When you feel something touching the back of your shoulder but you don't want to turn around? Have you ever felt like this before? I just did.

Holly Elizabeth Skelton (13)
South Hunsley School & Sixth Form College, North Ferriby

Always Running

All that could be heard was the constant pounding of my soles on the dirt path, matching the intense beating of my heart. My lungs were burning, but I couldn't stop now. He was here somewhere, hiding in the thick grey blanket of fog, stalking me the way a lioness stalks her prey. The sound of a twig breaking echoed around the monstrous trees, yet I didn't turn around. I just kept running. For one eerie moment, the only noise was my heavy breathing. Then suddenly, out of nowhere, a pair of heavy arms yanked me into a gloomy abyss...

Rebekah Flatt (13)
South Hunsley School & Sixth Form College, North Ferriby

Dystopian Nightmare

Located through the jet-black gates, was the daunting house. It silently stood still underneath the glistening moon, shining brightly. Obsidian coloured trees with nothing but cobwebs for leaves branched down overhanging. A destroyed cobblestone path led up to the rusted door clinging on by its hinges. Inside was a towering staircase, leading to an enormous room. Glancing out the broken sharp windows showed nothing but a spine-chilling graveyard. Gigantic chandeliers shoddily suspended. Thick air made it arduous to breathe. The plethora of dust strangled the room. The house was becoming annihilated. It was about to plummet to the ground.

Daniel Lutkin-Taylor (13)
South Hunsley School & Sixth Form College, North Ferriby

Vermilion

I stepped out of my house and immediately I knew something was wrong. The soft, gentle breeze was there, as was my house... But nothing else seemed to be the same. Flowers had appeared everywhere literally overnight and police patrolled the area. All I heard was the piercing sound of screeching sirens, like banshees in a bad mood; demolishing my eardrums... But then I saw why... An ambulance, a smashed car, a stretcher, a girl. Correction, a dead girl! Her hands were scarlet; the rest of her body, bloodshot. But I knew that face... The dead girl was me.

Jessica Kelly (13)
South Hunsley School & Sixth Form College, North Ferriby

The Mist

She should be dead! Curled up like a hibernating bear under the looming tree; branches scratched at her battered arms and back leaving unmerciful cuts. With a groan, she twitched, then lifted her arms to reveal many lumps of small insects feeding off her body. The grass pierced her skin. While in the distance, a mist swept towards the hopeless girl. 'Not again,' she whispered pleadingly. The mist was on top of her, clawing her crippled legs without mercy. Without warning, a hand pulled her into the mist. Screams echoed around before being sharply cut off... Nothing moved. Silence.

Daniel Haskins (13)
South Hunsley School & Sixth Form College, North Ferriby

Into The Drowning Mine

Lucy approached the rusty sluice gate slowly. She had heard strange noises the night before and curiosity had gotten the better of her. However, she had also heard stories of the old mine that it connected to; and how a sudden flood had drowned all 200 miners. Lucy was deep within the waterlogged tunnel, her torch swept shakily across the path ahead.

Splash! Lucy spun round, but nothing was there. There was another splash. Closer. She turned slowly around. Horror struck her face when a slimy amphibian-like hand dragged her underwater. Drowning screams echoed around the empty mine...

Adam Millard (14)

South Hunsley School & Sixth Form College, North Ferriby

Twisted

Something didn't seem right. The dense fog grew thicker and lurked for miles down the street. Ominous silhouettes danced around the mist, as I slowly stride through the mouth, into the heart of the deranged freak show. Still, ice-cold bodies hung from the ceiling, swinging in a motion. Disturbing music played from the stage, as the bloodstained curtains slowly opened, revealing a haunting scene behind. For much more than a moment, there was a menacing silence. So quiet, it pierced my eardrums. Suddenly, screams bellowed from backstage, and two horrific figures stood centre stage, laughing psychotically.

Bradley Phillip Groizard (13)

South Hunsley School & Sixth Form College, North Ferriby

What's At The End Of The Street?

At the end of the street is a house nobody dares go near. Everyone who had ever entered, never returned. There used to be a family who lived there, but all mysteriously disappeared, never to be seen again. Then one night at 3:15am, a light switched on in the attic window. But who turned on the light? Someone must be in there, but who? There is a legend that there is a demon girl who lives in the basement. She roams around at 3:15am, the time she was murdered! Who is at the end of the street? Who?

Kate Hirons (13)
South Hunsley School & Sixth Form College, North Ferriby

The Chase

A piercing screech echoed through the whole of the dark forest, followed by the rustles of leaves and eventually out of the bushes, sprinted a woman shrieking like her life depended on it. What she was running from was unknown at the moment, but she knew if she stopped, her life would be over, The light of the moon shone down, lighting the whole forest up. The woman shrieked for help with her phone out her pocket whilst diving into a bush. She was motionless as a cold hand rested on her shoulder...

Harry Catchpole (13)
South Hunsley School & Sixth Form College, North Ferriby

The Day They Came

29, 28, 27... I count down the seconds until they come to use my body, to destroy my mind. 19, 18, 17... I glance around the padded room, white with no escape and still, somehow, they find me every month on this exact day. 11, 10... I feel the shiver of death run through me and I open my mouth in a silent scream. No one will care, that's why I'm here, in a place for the insane. Every cell of my being rebels against the dark entity that slithers into my paralysed mind, and that's when the screaming starts...

Annalise Beharrell (14)

South Hunsley School & Sixth Form College, North Ferriby

The Raven

It swoops from shadow to shadow, merciless to its victims. Alive in the shadows; a silhouette in the light. It can only be seen in three places; the nightmares of the living, the dreams of the insane and the heartbeat before you die.

Always searching, never stopping; it will haunt you to your last breath and hear your dying shriek. After its visit you will be gone with no wisp of life left... No heartbeat... No warmth... Only your cold dead eyes. In return for your soul, the only trace of it being there is one of its black feathers...

Asher George Gallagher (13)

South Hunsley School & Sixth Form College, North Ferriby

Turning Corners

I'm finally here, finally at my grandma's house. And wow, it's pretty dark and daunting here. Oh well, I'm going in anyway. As a horrible feeling shivers down my spine, I walk into the ancient building and I call for my grandma, no reply. I see that there are two corners to turn, I decide to go right because there is an abnormal noise coming from the left. So I turn the corner and there seems to be more corners, I look back and the entrance is blocked. I continue going forward until...

Jack Marsh

South Hunsley School & Sixth Form College, North Ferriby

The Unusual Suspects' Dark Days!

Danger! I was in terrible danger. It was a matter of life or death; my family were worried that we might die. Earlier that day, a group of dangerous thugs and thieves came stomping into our house, threatening and shouting, demanding money. *'Give me your money you filthy animal or else I'll kill you!'* yelled one of the dangerous men. The thugs made pounding noises, destroying our flat.
Our neighbours, the Somersbys, had heard the pounding noise from next door. *Knock! Knock! Knock!* Pounding on the door was a loud noise. Who was it? Had they come to help us?

Morteza Afzali (13)

South Hunsley School & Sixth Form College, North Ferriby

It's Over!

Darkness; it surrounded me. All I could see was a vivid shape: fog emerged from the ground beneath me. A black figure lingered in the distance. Ribbed black cloths covered the ancient body. *Bang!* I looked towards the prehistoric building; huge cracked stone bricks made up the building. I crept towards it, my cold, slight hand reached out and grabbed the rusty handle, I turned it gradually and it creaked open. My head turned as I scanned the empty room. It was motionless. An icy hand touched my shoulder, then a voice croaked, 'It's over!' and the door slammed shut...

Loubie Stella Wright (13)

South Hunsley School & Sixth Form College, North Ferriby.

A Dark Night In December

I steadily clambered across the ragged rocks. A solitary silhouette stood, observing the soundless night. I flattened myself, hoping he hadn't noticed me. Who was he? Suddenly, he glided towards the ominous woods, glancing back only to hear the distant hoot of an owl. In my mind, I decided to follow him. I departed with haste into the gloomy wood after him. I searched the woods for any whisper of him. I heard a sharp howl arrive and disperse as quickly as it came. I heard a gentle whistle. Fearfully, I turned around. He whispered to me softly, 'Run!'

Dan Ward (14)

South Hunsley School & Sixth Form College, North Ferriby

The Day Everything Went Wrong

She shut the office door and stepped into the cold winter air. She opened her car door and leaned over and allowed herself to drop into the seat. Her hair was pinned up like perfection and her clothes looked like they had just been ironed. Then she took off, soon pulling into her drive. She pulled herself up, out of the car and crept up to the door. She inserted the key, gave it a twist, and entered the house ready for a relaxing night at home. She reached for the light switch, but a cold hand was already there...

Amy Louise Wood (13)
South Hunsley School & Sixth Form College, North Ferriby

Demonic Dreams

Dreams. Mostly they are just the product of a wild imagination. Although, there is a certain dream that is very infamous - a demonic vision. The plague of this world: it's worse than death and it can't end well. Ever. Its tyrannical spirits influencing all troubled minds in its path. These ghostly beings stare blankly at you with their blood-red eyes, each night creeping closer to your bedside. On the fifth night that these disturbing nightmares occur, the victim wakes with a start, finding sweat dripping from their palms. Then panic takes over. Bet your mind is troubled now...

Molly Wilson (12)
South Hunsley School & Sixth Form College, North Ferriby

Five Doors

I reached the ancient wooden door. The door opened into a pitch-black, spooky hallway. The lights were shattered. My body was as cold as an iceberg. I couldn't see my nervous fingers. There were five doors that surrounded my defenceless body. The five doors stared right through me. I had never heard such a high-pitched violent scream in my life. I had to pick a door, but which? I kept repeating in my head, *1, 2, 3, 4 or 5?* My life was flashing in front of my eyes until I realised it had to be door one...

Luke Antony Grimes (13)
South Hunsley School & Sixth Form College, North Ferriby

There's No Turning Back

The abandoned theme park suddenly sparked to life as you stepped through the old rusty gates. The sounds of fair rides filled the air with joy and happy memories of the past before the terrible accident. Then the gates slammed shut. You spun on your heel and dashed back to the gates, shaking them in an attempt to break free. You now realised there's no turning back. You decide to go further into the theme park. Then you hear a scream, you look all around you but there's no one there. But instead, you feel something breathing down your neck...

Megan Staniforth (13)
South Hunsley School & Sixth Form College, North Ferriby

Darkness

My eyes flash open but it makes no difference, it's as dark as black ink. How did I get here? My arms and legs refuse to move. Someone or something is making me stay. *Crack!* I struggle against my invisible bonds, determined to see. *Snap!* This time from the other side. I'm being penned in. Panic, delayed from whatever drug they gave me sets in. Blood-curdling screams pierce the night. I just realise they are coming from my mouth when a spidery white hand covers it. I feel a pain and then nothing. I know that this means I'm dead.

Ruby Franklin (13)
South Hunsley School & Sixth Form College, North Ferriby

The Mysterious Figure Of The Night

The aggressive wind howled like a hungry animal searching for its next victim. It sent spine-chilling shocks of fear down my terrified body. I headed out into the mystery of the night. Misty fog enclosed the church creating shadowing figures that lurked behind every corner. *Bang!* The door closed behind me. A rush of panic engulfed my body. Trees rustled against the cracked, cobwebbed windows. I heard an eerie whisper in my ear, 'Run.' The solitary word rang around in my ear, but there was nowhere to run, nowhere to hide. Would I escape the mysterious figure of the night?

Daisy Simpson (13)
South Hunsley School & Sixth Form College, North Ferriby

Lost

'Rufus! Here boy!' Dead leaves crunch beneath me. A shiver runs down my spine. Nobody's ever ventured this far into the dense forest. 'Rufus!' I yell frantically. Rustling comes from nearby. I whip around. 'Rufus?' From the shadows emerges a muscular body with straggly fur: black like its heart. Towering over me, glaring wildly with cold eyes. Razor teeth bared, I freeze against a twisted trunk as it approaches... Lost deep in the forest, I listen for my owner to call me again. No call comes. The sun cowers behind a cloud, casting darkness. That's when I hear her scream...

Eleanor Pearson (14)

South Hunsley School & Sixth Form College, North Ferriby

Silver

Fear. He looked at the girl, maybe 15 years old, stood opposite him. She was tall and slender with silver skin and short white hair. She wore a black mask which covered her entire face and held a bloody, razor-sharp knife that had recently come out of his leg. 'Hello Jack, I'm Silver, your worst nightmare,' she whispered, and rushed towards him. Jack tried and failed to run, collapsing from agony in his leg. Soon he'd be free from this torture, this pain. Screaming in agony, his vision faded as Silver leant over him. 'Ready for round 2, Jack?'

Lily Cleary (14)

South Hunsley School & Sixth Form College, North Ferriby

Nightmare On Elm Street

Chills radiated down her spine as she tiptoed down the dimly lit street. It was a concrete jungle with terrors peering around each corner. Speeding up, her steady walking pace transformed into a swift run. Running as fast as she could, she still felt followed. Daring to glance back, she could observe a masked figure menacingly cradling a machete. The street lights flickered eerily as if to tell her something was about to unfurl. Suddenly, all the lights cut out. She was alone. Unexpectedly, a cold hand grasped her shoulder then the owner whispered a solitary word, 'Run.'

Ben Adams
South Hunsley School & Sixth Form College, North Ferriby

A Gristly Tale

It was the winter of 1946 in Germany; everyone was hungry. In the main square, a frail man approached a plump, middle-aged woman. Coughing and spluttering the man requested, 'Could you please deliver this letter for me? The address is on the envelope.' The woman, of course, agreed to deliver the message. Whilst walking, the woman increasingly became curious as to what the letter read. Street by street, house by house, the address came into view; a butcher's shop. The woman's curiosity got the better of her, she opened the letter. It read, 'This is the last one today'...

William Carne (13)
South Hunsley School & Sixth Form College, North Ferriby

The Circus Of Death

The blood-curdling screams of their recent victims could be heard from miles away. Josh and his friends sneaked into the creepy, desolate, abandoned house. As they entered the dimly lit house, the battered wooden door slammed: sealing their fate. The walls were coated in the blood of the victims of the Amsterdam clowns. *Squeak, squeak, squeak*, the noise sounded more distant and increasingly quieter. Josh and his friends found some steps to the basement. As they went down the stairs, the lights fleetingly flickered, violently revealing the Amsterdam clowns with weapons in their hands ready to kill their victims.

Scott Wilson (13)
South Hunsley School & Sixth Form College, North Ferriby

Beneath The Shadows

Paul crept across the attic, the floor creaking. Then the candlelight blew out. 'Oh s- ,' Paul said like a coward. All Paul could hear was the distant noise of the wind. Then he saw in front, a candle, with a man. The window shut, the whole house turned pitch black. As he got nearer, the creaking of the floor got louder and louder. He looked behind, nothing. He called for his wife, nothing.
'Oh don't shout for help, she's gone,' laughed the man.
'Who the hell are you?' said Paul.
'I suffered,' said the man, 'so will you.'

James Burgess-Perez (13)
South Hunsley School & Sixth Form College, North Ferriby

Abandoned

Abandoned. My group just left me. I was lost. I was in a forest all by myself with no way out. It was like a maze with paths going left, right and straight down the middle. I kept on hearing noises like people stepping on branches around me. My heart was racing like I was about to win the 100m race. I felt a hand on my shoulder. I didn't dare turn around. Then a cold voice whispered, 'Run.' A shiver launched down my spine, making me unable to move. How could I escape... ?

Tom Dawson (14)
South Hunsley School & Sixth Form College, North Ferriby

Immune

Pulse violently racing, the mutation cornering me, death is upon me - the oblivion approaching fast! Sinking slowly, cowering as my mind is paralysed until - *bang!* In a split second, a bullet hits the creature in front of my defenceless body, consequently it falls backwards, smacking directly against the concrete floor! Dead, deceased, gone. A figure approaches from the haunting mist of the shadows; I gaze at my saviour. Lifting his hood slightly, he points the gun towards me. His palm steadies to pull the death machine's trigger, when suddenly a voice from deep inside me yells, 'No!'

Lucy Tessier (14)
South Hunsley School & Sixth Form College, North Ferriby

The Room

The man was standing outside the big abandoned castle. His arm hairs slowly rising upwards as he takes a step closer. He slowly turns the doorknob. As the door slowly creaks open, he takes a step inside. Everything is broken and rubbish is tipped all over the floor. He carefully begins to walk up the stairs, he hears a noise behind him. He turns around to find that a coffin has opened. He gets dragged upstairs by an unknown spirit. As he's getting dragged, his neck breaks on a splinter in the stairs.

Jake Morley (13)
South Hunsley School & Sixth Form College, North Ferriby

Disappear

A man walks into a church. He starts praying. 'Lord help me!' he screams.
'Boo!' a little girl says as she sits beside him.
'Argh!' he yells. The girl looks sad. 'I'm sorry. I didn't mean to be mean,' he quickly says.
'It's OK,' she whimpers, 'by the way, my name's Polly.'
'Umm, that's cool I suppose,' he shrugs, 'I'm Kevin.'
Suddenly, the lights go out for one second and then when they come back on, Polly's gone! They flicker again as Kevin is in front of a mirror and he realises he's disappeared too!

Anna Downey (13)
South Hunsley School & Sixth Form College, North Ferriby

A Stormy Stir!

Louise was laid in bed one night. The wind was howling and there was a storm. She had no parents; she was an orphan. Her room was at the top, in the attic. There was a hole in the roof, so every night she would look up at the stars! But tonight was different because there was a storm. Louise lay in bed shivering, trying to make herself warm. She was scared because she could hear footsteps creeping around her room. She hid under her covers, it was pitch-black. Someone whispered, 'Death is upon you.' Louise screamed...

Bella Levitt (12)
South Hunsley School & Sixth Form College, North Ferriby

The End Of The Road

As the boy sauntered through the dark, mystic street, the bushes started to rumble and shake. The illuminated moon peeked over the tree line and up into the sky. It lit up what looked like a deserted street. As the child walked, so did the reminiscence of his mind. It chased him and wouldn't leave him. It took his mind off what was actually happening all around him. Creeping and crawling, running and sprinting, yet he did not realise he reached the end of the road physically and mentally; opening his eyes to what was right in front of him...

Harrison Norton (13)
South Hunsley School & Sixth Form College, North Ferriby

Nightfall On The Moors

Nightfall was coming, I stumbled through the snowy hills when I caught a glimpse of fog creeping down the uneven pathways. The fog surrounded me like an unearthly mist. I descended eagerly, not wanting to be alone here. Clumps of pink heather broke through the snow, suddenly my foot caught on something, I knelt down to free it. Behind me I heard a *pitter-patter* of feet on the snow, I turned but no one was to be seen. My heart pounded fast and my mouth felt dry, 'Keep calm,' I breathed, I hurried my steps and prayed for help...

Fabian Woodward (13)
South Hunsley School & Sixth Form College, North Ferriby

A Race Against Time

Escape... It was the only option. She knew. Afraid, she knew why she needed to get out - but how? Desperately, she searched her mind for a plan - a sensible plan - to escape from the deserted surroundings. She was in here for one reason: for protection, but this time, she wasn't protected, she was in danger. Her mind raced, shivers were sent down her spine. Her time was up. She felt a bitterly cold hand on her shoulder. A deep voice called out, 'It's over.' Shadows circled her. 'You can't escape now.'

Abbie Williams (13)
South Hunsley School & Sixth Form College, North Ferriby

The Phantom

The girls both strolled up the uneven, pebbly, crooked path to the old church. Both of the girls stopped in front of the big oak door and stared in shock, they felt like they were being watched by the souls that loomed outside, and the clouds that covered the moon. They stepped inside.

The room was becoming darker and light started to dim. A crack of lightning struck the night sky, shadows crept up the walls. Suddenly, the lights went out. A blood-curdling scream came from where Katie was stood. The lights came back on. Katie was gone.

Cody-May Whitehead (11)
South Hunsley School & Sixth Form College, North Ferriby

Home Sweet Home

Everything was safe. The door was tightly bolted; the chain was securely hooked. Comfortable lounging inside of my duck-feather duvet, all warm and toasty in my house, not even doubting my sanctuary's security. My own haven, home sweet home. Yet tonight felt different. Tonight was the first night I noticed the noises outside. Every creak gave me a heart attack and soon I was hidden underneath my pillow. Just as I began to laugh, I heard a noise. A sort of thud. Like someone coming up the stairs. One thud, two thuds, three thuds, four... five... six... seven... Silence.

Callie Ball (13)
South Hunsley School & Sixth Form College, North Ferriby

Shadow

Music blaring. Voice singing, body dancing. Staring into the mirror, watching the reflection. Light shines in my blue room. Blue bed, blue wall, blue dresser, black shadow, blue curtains. Wait... black shadow? Cautiously turning around, there is no one there. Weird. Just my imagination. Going back to dancing, I feel a presence. Just my imagination. Carrying on dancing, I steal a few glances around the room. Just my imagination. There's no one here. When I look to the mirror, terror courses through me. Black shadow. Just my imagination. Just my imagination.

Jolie Bull (13)
South Hunsley School & Sixth Form College, North Ferriby

The House Of Disappearance

No one dared go near the house on top of the hill. There had been disappearances there almost every week, each person last seen heading up the hill to the next village. As I got closer, the image of the house silhouetted in the dark sky edges into view. Many windows were smashed, dark green moss peeled off the wall, dead trees stood in the garden and rain hammered down on the half demolished roof. A shiver ran down my spine. A cold, dead hand grabbed me, covering my mouth and eyes...

Ben Hindson (13)
South Hunsley School & Sixth Form College, North Ferriby

The Unknown Realm

Silence. The shattered world around me was decaying. The lures of the ancient order had destroyed the treaty, leaving civilization for inevitable doom. Fate had brought me here, but what was the cause? All these questions but no answers. Ruins lay about like my fragmented memories. How did I get here? Questions flooded into me like the gush of a waterfall. This world obliterated the laws of reality, or at least what I thought it was. Annihilation was the one word frazzling my mind. I knew this was no coincidence, I brought myself here, but why? This was the end.

Jamie Matthews (13)
South Hunsley School & Sixth Form College, North Ferriby

The Red Forest

It was cold, the sky darkened and the grass grew red. A thick fog gloomed over my feet and a howl came from in the trees. The forest darkness grew on me like a plague and the grey thorns pierced my skin like knives sharpened by bones. The wind blew and shadows flew around me. Whispers came from the bushes like Alcatraz prison. There was no escape from this horror. Then snapping twigs came from behind me, the sound got louder and soon whatever it was had gotten so close I could smell rotting flesh. A shadow grew on me...

Charlie Revell (13)
South Hunsley School & Sixth Form College, North Ferriby

Dusk 2 Dawn

Vroom! The engine stopped. I called the car company for help - no reply. I got out of the van and searched for society. I found a little corner shop, *Dusk 2 Dawn*. I entered. As the light flickered, something flew past me. I froze. The strange figure was hovering two metres above the ground, she had no face. I woke up, it was just a dream. I went to comb my hair, then, in the mirror, I realised I was the faceless one...

Dylan Shaffi (11)
South Hunsley School & Sixth Form College, North Ferriby

Curse

The bullet tore through my flesh like a needle to a balloon. I fell to the ground as my life slowly slipped away. My friends stared upon my body in shock. I eventually died of blood loss from the gaping hole in my left lung. But then I woke up in my bed, wearing my same old clothes, the blood now gone. I went to school the next day. My friends walked up to me, oblivious to my death the previous day. I left wearing my orange parka, alone and depressed. No one could ever understand my curse. No one.

Caleb Canet-Baldwin (11)
South Hunsley School & Sixth Form College, North Ferriby

The Forest Was Alive

The tree's branches were menacing claws, reaching out to me, haunting me: as I walked onwards through the gloomy labyrinth of crinkling leaves, my paranoid emotions were increasing drastic. The moon was a ghostly galleon among the black sea known as the sky. The midnight mist hiding who knows what? An enemy? A predator? Owls hooting, wolves howling, it seems I am not alone in these woods. And of course, my constant companion, the driving force swaying the horrors in this place. The wind. Its howling claws prickling my neck. The forest was alive.

Alexander White (11)
South Hunsley School & Sixth Form College, North Ferriby

The Ouija Board

Memories haunted him as he arrived at his parents' ski lodge. His friends were already there. He was glad he was there, in remembrance of his sisters who went missing there.

As the night grew darker, things became more and more spooky. Then Chris came up with the dreadful idea, a Ouija board. Josh quickly crept into the damp, dusty basement and found the old Ouija board. An hour of unanswered questions passed... *Bang!* Everybody yelped and jumped up. The door flew open. Slowly, the two dead sisters entered, in synchronisation. 'You did this to us,' they slowly bellowed...

Annie Chappell (13)
South Hunsley School & Sixth Form College, North Ferriby

The Corridor Of Horror

Creak! I walked down the corridor, I tiptoed over the old, broken floorboards. As I got further down the corridor, I heard a *pitter-patter* getting louder and louder. At the end of the corridor, a shadow appeared from nowhere. I looked at the figure as it looked back at me. I was petrified as the cold, dark eyes stared into my soul. I slowly staggered backwards up against a wall, the figure moving closer and closer. Suddenly, the figure vanished into thin air. Then I felt a cold, bony hand tap me on the shoulder...

Adam Bell (14)
South Hunsley School & Sixth Form College, North Ferriby

The Axecutioner

Cold, damp and wet, the wind was howling through the thickness of the fog. Camp Windemere was surrounded by masses of sinister trees. Fawn and I were so bored that we decided to do dares. *The isolated shack*, I thought! The perfect dare. I told Fawn my idea, she agreed.
As we stumbled outside our cabin, we noticed a message carved into the stump of a tree, 'He's coming!' The winds were picking up and the dark figures in the forest were getting close. I turned around to hear Fawn's scream echo in the distance. I realised... I was next...

Leah Dalee (11)
South Hunsley School & Sixth Form College, North Ferriby

'Her'

I stood up, shuffling on my slippers and walking quickly to the door, but just as I got close it slammed shut, scaring the living daylights out of me and making me stumble to the ground. I whimpered. 'Cassssie,' a weird doll voice sang out, sending chills up my spine.

'Leave me alone!' I cried, bringing my legs up to my chest and burying my head into them.

'Let's play.'

My eyes suddenly shot open in fear. The aura that filled the room was heavy and fearful. I could feel *her* watching me, *her* taunting voice beckoning me to play.

Chloe Louise Robinson (13)
South Hunsley School & Sixth Form College, North Ferriby

Death In The Side Street!

Midnight in the city of New York. Dead silence is occurring, everyone's asleep but one - John. Lacking sleep, every single night he dreads nightmares and goes for wanders. But tonight is different...

Hours passed by and John got sleepy, then left and finally walked down an alleyway, the alleyway of death.

Signs were everywhere saying, *Death Spot* or *Death Street* and whispers, (maybe young men like John as guards), saying, 'Go back,' constantly, but then... *Splat!* He was never seen again.

Charlie Lennard-White (11)
South Hunsley School & Sixth Form College, North Ferriby

The House

I crept through the old, mysterious graveyard until a tall, black gate stood in front of me! I leaned on it and peered through at the gothic mansion inside completely covered with ivy. The gate opened and I fell through. I tried to turn back but the gate clanged shut. I had no choice but to walk forwards!

I got to the house and opened the old, rusty door. My heart was in my mouth as I stepped inside the cobweb-filled mansion. 'Hello?' I bellowed into the darkness. I turned around, there was a hand on my shoulder...

Shannon Blood (13)
South Hunsley School & Sixth Form College, North Ferriby

Let Me Out!

'What was that?' cried Alex. Danny sniggered as the moonlight shone down on their faces like a pebble on a sandy beach. They dashed past the reception and into the first room down the hallway. It was a padded cell containing a torn straight jacket lying discarded in a corner. Suddenly, their attention switched to a sharp clang outside of the cell. Danny gave a nervous laugh as he turned to see Alex's face drained of all colour. 'Where is the jacket?' stuttered Alex. Without thinking, they bolted towards the door, only to find - they were trapped!

Lily Kendall (11)
South Hunsley School & Sixth Form College, North Ferriby

The Tuppenny Murderers

'And this,' came a cold voice behind the boy, 'is Alice, the Bloodstained Princess.' Edward could hear the strained, barely kept back insanity in his captor's words. 'Your new mistress.' Edward gulped and looked up. He gasped.

The child was breathtakingly beautiful. Long, straight, almost platinum-blonde hair cascaded down her back. Pale porcelain skin that glowed in the moonlight. She was like a china doll. She smiled at him, and he vaguely wondered how such a sweet child was a killer. Her red and blue eyes glittered like a snake's. Alice walked up to him. 'Welcome home... big brother.'

Isabeau Merena Cousins (13)
South Hunsley School & Sixth Form College, North Ferriby

The Head

A girl called Sudi was all by herself walking towards the house. Suddenly, the rain was pouring like the waves had crashed together. She had no choice but to go in. Before she entered, she saw a sign saying, *If you dare to enter, you can never come out,* but the wind was howling and roaring so she had to go in. One step in, the door banged, *bang!* The lights went off, luckily, she had a bag which had a torch but the torch had no batteries. Softly, she fainted.

In the morning, all she saw was a head!

Sudipthi Saravanan (11)
South Hunsley School & Sixth Form College, North Ferriby

The Babysitter

It was a dark, cold night when Mr and Mrs Greenacre went out for tea and left their child with a babysitter! It was about 7:30pm when David started to get hungry so he asked his babysitter for some food and she said, 'No!' About an hour later, he asked again and she shouted, 'No!' At about 9pm, he was so hungry, he sneaked into the kitchen and filled himself with chocolate, his babysitter's chocolate! As he turned to go back to his bed, his babysitter was stood behind him with a sharp, bloody knife... !

Ben Harrison (11)
South Hunsley School & Sixth Form College, North Ferriby

She Didn't Know

For some unexplainable reason, she felt safe here; she knew no one else had ever visited; she knew no one else would. Subsequently, she didn't know. She didn't know what they all knew. The silence within the atmosphere was deafening. Light bled through cuts in the fearful, abandoned window. Life in this half-dead room was non-existent. Despite the eerie atmosphere and the malicious damage, she felt safe here; her own cocoon, like a butterfly. Midnight, clock chimed, 'Hello?' Her voice was trepidatious, her hands shaking.
2am, a charcoal silhouette healed bleeding cuts in the window. Bitter hands grasped her shoulders...

Jemma Cottam (13)
South Hunsley School & Sixth Form College, North Ferriby

The Graveyard

Fog was creeping in. I felt a freezing hand on my leather coat. A wave of shock struck me. All of a sudden, I turned around sharply, no one there. I felt breathing on my neck. My heart skipped a beat. A million thoughts rushed through my head; vampire? Werewolf? Ghost? Demon? All of a sudden, I heard the roaring noise of a car engine. As quick as a flash I turned, but only to see my car driving away... I screamed for it to stop, it did. I ran to get in but I heard, 'Leaving so soon?' Terrifying.

Lucy Maddison (14)
South Hunsley School & Sixth Form College, North Ferriby

The Man In The Shadow

It was cold and gloomy, the sun was slowly going down and the rays cast elegant shadows upon the ground. My eyes pierced to the floor. I noticed a shadow that looked just like a man holding a gun of some sort, but as I looked up, I noticed that there was nobody there. The shadow's arm slowly rose, along with the gun. I ran, but at every corner, they were there. 'Who are you?' I shouted. *Bang!* A shadow of a bullet left the gun's barrel with great force. I glanced down, droplets of blood fell to my hand...

Sam Luca Furniss
South Hunsley School & Sixth Form College, North Ferriby

Blood-Red

The car pulled up to the dark drive of Motel End. I had the feeling of adrenaline rushing through my veins. I twisted the rusty doorknob of room thirteen and pushed the door open smoothly. The repulsive snores of the stupid twit pierced my ears. I pulled the silver, glimmering knife out as I stood over the blind victim. The metal slit his soft, pale neck. I lifted the blade up and walked out slowly. The clicking of my blood-red stilettos sounded on the concrete. I had just killed my husband, and did I like it? Yes I did.

Beth Giblin
South Hunsley School & Sixth Form College, North Ferriby

The Phone Box

On a dark, raging, stormy night, a man called Bailey walked into a telephone box and straight to his sight, he saw four very large scratches which looked as big as a dinosaur claw. The man picked up the phone and called the taxi place; he said, 'I'm looking for a taxi at Downfield Lane.' And to his surprise, he heard a really frightening scream, 'Argh!' Then a man with a rather deep, creepy voice said, 'Ha ha I wouldn't stay there for long!' Bailey started to run away, when out of nowhere a cold hand touched his shivering shoulder...

Bailey Fairfield (12)
South Hunsley School & Sixth Form College, North Ferriby

School

It was just a normal day until Miss Phillips came. Miss Phillips was a vile woman and she deserved everything she got. It was midday, about 4:30pm when we had to come back for a detention. We were about halfway through the detention when my friend got taken out of the room. Then after that I never saw him again. Then suddenly, Miss came back in and said it was my turn.
She took me to a dark room and then *bang!* I never saw my family again. Miss Phillips got killed the day after.

Will Rands (14)
South Hunsley School & Sixth Form College, North Ferriby

Hiding Beneath The Darkness

After all the times I've been there for her. After everything we've been through together. Everything's over now. Now she's left me...
Wistful church bells chimed as the darkness drifted down the aisle; watched on by inconsolable crowds. Standing nervously at the back, I listened to the cries of mourners next to me; forever wishing I hadn't. Beneath the vibrant stained-glass windows, stood a disconsolate man with a solemn expression on his face; staring straight into my eyes! Slowly, I strolled quietly out of the dead church, aware of the depressing ceremony ahead of me. His eyes on me.

Cameo Jefferson (14)
South Hunsley School & Sixth Form College, North Ferriby

Trepidation

The weather was fierce. Shaking; I crept into the dark, abandoned, derelict building. Rain crashed down the rusty, unstable windows. Nervously, I sat on the dusty, red, uncomfortable chair. Suddenly, there was movement. A rocking chair started rocking frantically. But… it was empty. I gulped. It carried on frantically rocking. Frightened for my life, I got up. I tried to leave, but the door was jammed. I gulped again. What could I do? In despair, I tried again. My heart stopped, I put all effort in trying to bang down the door. Then I heard a voice. It was over…

Tom Harris (13)
South Hunsley School & Sixth Form College, North Ferriby

The Good Samaritan

She knew it was a mistake, a big mistake. It all began on the night of Halloween when her best friend was silenced. It was a cold, foggy night in October and Lilly strolled happily towards Swanland Church. She should have known better. He was waiting, waiting patiently. His thick leather gloves closed around the heavy rope lurking in his pocket. However, an old man stepped in front of Lilly. She jumped then relaxed when she saw it was a kindly, silver-haired gentleman. She smiled. He smiled. She giggled. He giggled, as his fist clenched around the heavy rope…

Laura Battams (13)
South Hunsley School & Sixth Form College, North Ferriby

Hickory Dickory Dock

The last thing I remember is being curled up in bed, safe. Then I felt the chains tying around me, forcing me upright. I opened my eyes to see my own personal hell; disfigured bodies strung up on the wall, bloody and lifeless. I screamed, making my throat sore. I heard a clock strike twelve, drowning out my voice. Millions of spiders crawled around my body. I quivered and forced my mouth shut. On the last chime, I felt a sting. I forced open my eyes. It was just a dream. Then I saw the spider bites on my arm...

Grace Ellis (11)
South Hunsley School & Sixth Form College, North Ferriby

A Labyrinth In A Maze

Kidan was batted away, hitting the stone-cold wall with a hefty thud. Anything could have hit him but, slowly opening his eyes, a tall, dark centaur stood in his path.
'What are you doing here hero?'
Kidan came to his feet and screamed, 'I want my friend back!'
The centaur hit him again but much harder, he went through the wall. All of a sudden, the maze grew hotter, Kidan had to figure a way out before being burnt to a crisp. He found a small chamber with a sphinx in it.
'Answer my question, your wish is granted.'

Marcus Finlay Thacker (14)
South Hunsley School & Sixth Form College, North Ferriby

Last Words

Silhouettes of the lifeless trees sent cold shivers down my spine, as I crept through the daunting and looming graveyard towards the front iron gates. As the hairs on the back of my neck spiked my clothing, my heart raced as I ran in-between the old and decrepit gravestones. I could make out a ghastly, mysterious figure. Fumbling, I quickly tried to undo the latch of the gate. 'Hello,' a weary voice sounded, I stopped what I was doing. My heart was pounding and it was hurting my chest. Apprehensively, I muttered, 'Callum, is that you?' The silence was ear-piercing...

Joshua Wilcox

South Hunsley School & Sixth Form College, North Ferriby

The Curious

Apprehensively, the curious girl crept towards the ageing cabin. Towering trees surrounded her. Aside from her fear, eagerness for exploration urged her forward. Once she reached the weathered door with rusty hinges, she gradually unlatched it and sneaked inside. She peered into the gloom like an owl intent for movement from its prey. Abruptly, a shattering shriek emerged. The now fearful girl sharply eyed the overwhelming space. Another bitter scream echoed so she headed towards the exit. An ice block grabbed her and hauled her to the centre of the room. She yelped dramatically but the hand muffled her voice...

Naomi Brailsford (13)

South Hunsley School & Sixth Form College, North Ferriby

You're Kidding, Right?

'You're kidding right? I'm not spending a night in there.'
I looked at the abandoned asylum. Fear crept up my back.
'Dude, it's only a night,' Lily laughed.
'Fine!' I regrettably agreed.
We trudged up the worn-out path to the non-existent door.
'Maybe we should go back,' I spoke cowardly.
'No you will not leave!' I stumbled back in surprise.
'Lily?'
'No, this is Raphael!' she growled as she picked me up by the throat.
'Lily stop!' She dropped me and I ran for my life.

Two years later, the phone rang.
'Hello?' I asked.
'Hey Sammy, this is Raphael... '

Rebecca Lidster (13)
South Hunsley School & Sixth Form College, North Ferriby

The Woods

The leaves rustled at my feet. I shivered. 'Phil... Phil!' I lumbered
through the all-consuming mud. *Squelch, squelch*. A limb appeared
in the leaves. 'Phil?' I whispered. Gradually, the wind subsided, the
leaves uncovered a leg, then a head... and then I discovered, it was
Phil. A shadowy figure revealed himself from the misty fog. I was
too busy mourning my lost friend to notice the man. I turned. The
spinning blades were the final sight of my life...

Harry James Mitchell (14)
South Hunsley School & Sixth Form College, North Ferriby

The Stalker

I heard a squeak and turned around. Nothing. Darkness. I started walking faster, my house was in sight. I almost started running. Another squeak sound followed by a cruel, evil laugh. I sprinted towards my house. 'You can't escape me.' I looked around to see where the voice came from. 'Keep running.' My legs started moving faster and faster, but I couldn't reach the house in time. 'You can't escape me.' With tears running down my cheeks, I stopped. Was this an alarm? Was I dreaming?
'I will always be right beside you my love, even in your dreams. Always.'

Emma Garland (13)
South Hunsley School & Sixth Form College, North Ferriby

The Shadow

It was a cold, spine-tingling evening. There was tension in the air. Tom and Jenny entered the church, the light was dimmed and their footsteps echoed. Every time Tom took a footstep there was an echo. He just thought to himself, *it must just be Jenny,* but was it? Every time Jenny took a step there was an echo. She thought to herself, *it must be Tom.* There was a *bang!*
'Tom, is that you?'
'Jenny, is that you?'
There was a hand on her shoulder.
'Tom, is that you… ?'

William Jones (13)
South Hunsley School & Sixth Form College, North Ferriby

Horrid House

I walk past this house every day when walking home; it's creepy, very creepy. It's a dark, tall and thin house. I never see who is in it. But on this one day, I saw them as soon as I had gone past. It was a lady; an old lady. She was in full black clothes and had her head down. The next day I waited for her, I then asked her, 'Why do you not want me to see you?'

'Because I'm ugly.'

She ran off straight away. Since that day I have never ever seen that lady again...

Matthew Harrison (14)

South Hunsley School & Sixth Form College, North Ferriby

Not Alone

Crash! Bang!

The rocks fall, 'No!' I scream. That's my only way out. It was only supposed to have been a silly dare to enter the old mine, but now I'm buried alive. I start to frantically pull at the jagged rocks, but they won't move. I screech for help: but what's the chance of someone passing this abandoned, isolated place? I scratch at the earth to escape until my fingers bleed.

'Help, please, anyone,' I cry.

'You're never getting out of this place,' comes an eerie voice from the blackness.

It is then that I know I'm not alone...

Emily Just (13)

South Hunsley School & Sixth Form College, North Ferriby

Satan's Servants

The last train pulls into the empty station. Funny: it looks like one of those old-fashioned steam trains. Nonetheless, it's a train.
I board, finding an empty carriage. I sit down, chilly under the open window. It starts off and everything begins. Voices wailing and shadows dancing. No figures to cast the shadows but shadows getting closer and closer to me. Soon after, it turns freezing and all the lights on this horror express go out and I am submerged in darkness.
I wake up with a cry, I'm back on the train: shadows. My dreams are real...

Hayden Dower (13)
South Hunsley School & Sixth Form College, North Ferriby

Sleepless Nights

My sweetest sensation cocooned me like a caterpillar before beauty. It was then I knew I was safe. Safe in a place I adored. A place when I was silent - it was silent. My body indulged; I was dragged into my harmless sleep, disturbing the silence around me. My curiosity could finally explode. Abandoned I felt, as I looked around the unlit room. I clamoured... But all that replied was the eerie silence. A cold hand gripped my arm, however nothing was there. I was not alone. Inadequate, wistful thoughts ran through my mind. Death had crossed my path!

Jess Park (14)
South Hunsley School & Sixth Form College, North Ferriby

Tandoori Chicken

Last night, my friend and I had just come in from a night out. We arrived at my apartment giggling and laughing, about to put on a film, when she suddenly said, 'Tandoori chicken.' You can imagine my confusion when she said this. 'Tandoori chicken, I want some now.' It was about 12am and she was insisting on having chicken.
'I'll order it online.'
'No! I'll get it myself.'
She barged outside.
'Someone's under your bed.'
Later that night the police came; he had been under there for at least 3 months, watching my every move!

Darcy Robinson (12)
South Hunsley School & Sixth Form College, North Ferriby

The Alleyway

Bob roamed through the predawn hazy fog; his peacock-feathered collar from his jacket hung loosely around his bitter, young cheeks and brisk neck. Either side of him were walls - walls of an abandoned alleyway. He stopped. A meagre twitch in his ear. There was a sound: a boot on cobblestone perhaps? The vast blanket of murky morning fog diminished his ability of hearing; he became anxious. He turned abruptly. There lurked a towering shadow below him, it seemed to stalk his every move. The sea of fog whisked around his legs. 'Hello?' A cold hand grasped his arm...

James Cheng (14)
South Hunsley School & Sixth Form College, North Ferriby

The Knocker

Have you heard about The Knocker? Maybe, maybe not. If you haven't, I hope this will make you think. If he knocks twice for you, then you are marked for death. Three knocks will send you insane. Four will kill you.

You will see him slowly, slowly shuffling towards you, arms outstretched. I've heard him, I remember the fear! The final knock made the world go black as my heart thudded to a stop. You may wonder how I am telling this story. Well, I didn't die - not quite. I became another Knocker... and I'm coming...

Knock, knock, knock.

Olivia Betts (12)
South Hunsley School & Sixth Form College, North Ferriby

Seeing Things...

A new house, a new start and a new beginning, me and my family moved into our new house. But I never expected to start seeing things... The first night in my new bedroom was terrible, it was damp and cold. But what was really scary was a glowing white figure that had dark circles for eyes and a grey oval, supposedly the mouth. Then the night after, the glowing figure was only a few inches away from me - its eyes were dark portals trying to transport me to my doom, I knew I wasn't seeing things...

Jess Wickett (12)
South Hunsley School & Sixth Form College, North Ferriby

The Beast

John Iravelled through the horrifying forest, desperately gasping for air. He kept on running as the monstrosity sprinted after him, John's heart pounded as it was filled with fear, he stopped, looking for a way out of this situation, a road was spotted in the distance, John hoped the road would lead him to safety. He was at the road but so was the beast. *Swoosh!* The extraterrestrial monster had gone, John walked home quivering and eyes full of tears, but he did not realise they were to meet again, only the next time was John's last. John disappeared forever.

Alfred George Johnson (14)
South Hunsley School & Sixth Form College, North Ferriby

Into The Woods

The night was upon us. As we moved through the woods, the wind was whistling around us. The abandoned house crept towards us, we had no idea what we faced. I went to open the door. I wriggled the handle until the door came loose, it was as if someone was behind us, creeping up. The fog followed us in like a hunting fox stalking its prey. We moved swiftly, checking for anyone or anything. I stopped. 'Jack!' I shouted, 'Jack?' He was gone. I stepped backwards, then I felt it. A hand which tightened fiercely around my neck...

Oliver Ingram (14)
South Hunsley School & Sixth Form College, North Ferriby

Run!

My legs ached as I pulled my strength together to sprint. It was getting dark and I seemed to be getting nowhere. I thought the walls were closing in... I needed to find Jack's house, *I think I found it!* I rubbed my eyes and ran forwards. I went in... The door shut behind me and locked itself. I heard music from the attic, it brought back a flashback of me and Jack playing with a doll. Suddenly, I heard Jack shriek... I ran towards him but tripped over a loose floorboard and landed on Jack... Dead Jack.

Rafferty Morland (11)
South Hunsley School & Sixth Form College, North Ferriby

Doll House... !

Last year, my family and I rented a house by a lake. As I unpacked, I came across a china doll. Her eyes were midnight-blue marbles and her lips were as red as blood and her hair was soft and silky.
The first night, I placed her on my dresser and went to sleep. The next morning she was at the foot of my bed. I rubbed my eyes and she was gone.
The next night, I sat her on my chair. In the morning she was next to me, on my bed, staring into my dark hazel eyes...

Eleanor Gratrix (12)
South Hunsley School & Sixth Form College, North Ferriby

The Thing

The bitter cold winter night gave Mike a chill down the spine.
Fog crawled around the forest like a hunting fox. The soft crunch
underneath the foot, not a reassuring sound. Wrapped tightly, he
approached the factory after pursuing his friend's horrifying call. His
dimmed yellow flashlight led the way. Not knowing what to expect,
Mike ventured in... A deafening scream burst the eardrums. The
flashlight bursting the bulb. As he entered the deep darkness of the
factory, a gust of wind stroked the cheek. Mike ran, looking behind.
The bright glow of the exit light gave Mike hope, then...

Alistair Hall (13)
South Hunsley School & Sixth Form College, North Ferriby

The Cabin In The Woods

There was a man walking through the forest, he really needed the
toilet. He said to his mates, 'Do you know where there is a toilet?'
They replied, 'No.' He looked to his left and saw a cabin... He went
over and knocked on the door, no answer. He tried the handle, it
worked.
He went to the loo, as he came back he heard a gunshot. *Bang,
bang, bang!* He went over to the window and saw his friends... He got
really, really scared, he nearly started crying. He looked next to him
and he saw a gun...

Josh Smith (11)
South Hunsley School & Sixth Form College, North Ferriby

The End

Thick grey fog crept steadily over the Kirk's dilapidated cross, while the electric hurricane tore the rotting flesh off the skeletons which lay scattered on the sacred ground. Echoes of thunder rippled across the black, inky sky and the salty wind tore violently through the dim atmosphere causing a burning, icy shiver down the back of the dead corpse which lay paralysed underground. As the lightning snapped the brittle twigs in half on the Arctic land, a booming crack between our wretched world and the land of the dead had opened. Creating the start of the Earth's miserable end.

Evie Sallis (14)
South Hunsley School & Sixth Form College, North Ferriby

The Hand

She was alone that night. Outside, the floor was covered with snow. From the corner of her eye, she spotted a dark figure in her garden. Panicking, she ran upstairs and locked herself in her room. She sat silently, her heart racing. After what felt like forever, she daringly peered out of the window. She didn't see anything. Silently, she tiptoed out of the room and down the stairs. Apprehensively, she approached the window. She spotted the figure, and it was edging nearer. She looked down only to see no footprints. She felt a hand touch her from behind...

Robert Stephen Bower (14)
South Hunsley School & Sixth Form College, North Ferriby

The 5th Of November

It all happened on the 5th of November! Michael slowly tiptoed into the abandoned house... The darkness simmered over the spooky house as I took another minuscule step! Even though I was trying to be quiet, the menacing creature could still hear my tiptoeing feet against the creaky floorboard. Out of the blue, a creature pounced for my waist and missed by a millimetre. He pounced again and this time he got my wrinkly neck and kept on clinging on... My neck started to ooze with blood. I examined the creature and then started to yank it off me.

Nathan Murrey (13)
South Hunsley School & Sixth Form College, North Ferriby

Lost

She was lost. Jenny was wandering in the woods, trying to escape. The rain poured down, soaking the soil. She trekked through the leaves, her pace quickened. Twigs kept snapping, leaves were rustling. Her heartbeat quickened. She raced to the edge of the woods. Finally, she reached a clearing. Stood in the distance, was a rickety, abandoned house. Jenny reached the broken door, all soaked and freezing. As the door swung open, she drifted inside. Gusts of wind slammed the door closed behind her and brushed past her. Something pushed Jenny to aside. *Bang!* It came from the kitchen. 'Hello?'

Hollie Ann Preston (14)
South Hunsley School & Sixth Form College, North Ferriby

Eternal Forest

Lost. All alone in a dark forest. I could here ominous sounds echoing all around me. There was only a little starlight to light my way through the forest. I must have been walking for days in the same direction before I collapsed. I woke up in chains, standing before me a strange man that looked dead and covered in blood. Next to me was a pile of corpses all killed the same way, drained of all life and blood. I realised I was next. *Slash*. The scream echoed through the eternal forest where the dead murderer lived.

Lucy Parkes (13)
South Hunsley School & Sixth Form College, North Ferriby

The Scream

It was a dark and dusty night and a boy of only ten was lost in a pitch-black forest with only his torch to guide him through this terrifying night. Suddenly, he heard a noise, he had no idea what it was. There it was again, it was going in a loop now. The noises were surrounding him, just then a wolf crept out a bush and was staring at him, not concentrating on anything else, just him. He ran. He ran into the woods, not caring which way anymore, and more wolves appeared. Then a scream rang out...

Jacob Ward (11)
South Hunsley School & Sixth Form College, North Ferriby

The Haunter

Graham awoke in an instant. An eerie ringing went through the house as darkness surrounded him. He unwillingly opened his rose curtains and peered round the mahogany post. As he was a cheapskate he couldn't be bothered to light his lamps.

Chink.

'Hello?' cried Graham.

Chink. The sound grew louder.

'Who's there?'

Chink, chink!

A ghostly blue glow started to appear around the corner. Graham fiercely shut his curtains and sat in the middle of his bed, covered by his sheets. The glow started to pierce the curtains' barrier. A gradual finger began to appear through the curtains' break point...

Alistair Marshall (11)

South Hunsley School & Sixth Form College, North Ferriby

The Night At The Graveyard

One day, late at night, the boys were playing hide-and-seek. One boy on his own hid under a bush in the graveyard.

Once all of the boys got bored they met up outside the graveyard but the boy who hid in the bush in the graveyard wasn't there. Every minute the other boys could hear a shriek from the bush...

But at one point, the shriek stopped and it began to get foggy. The boys saw a shadow and it was the other boy, but he wasn't there...

'Argh, argh, what is it? Where is it? He's back... '

George Todd (11)

South Hunsley School & Sixth Form College, North Ferriby

The Ava-Cado Monster

One day, a group of friends were playing out then suddenly a very pale-skinned girl appeared out of the darkness and said, 'I'm Ava-Cado.' The friends stared in amazement as Ava-Cado disappeared in a flash of smoke.

The next day, Ava-Cado reappeared, one of the friends was eating an avocado then Ava-Cado turned into a hideous monster and devoured all of the five friends, none of them were ever seen again. Rumour has it that the friends and Ava-Cado roam that very street...

Sophie Walker (12)
South Hunsley School & Sixth Form College, North Ferriby

The Christmas Killer

It's Christmas Eve, people are enjoying themselves laughing, joking except one person, the masked killer. Every Christmas, he kills somebody, his last victim was a helpless old lady who had no idea what was happening.

No lights on in his house, he begins planning how to kill his next victim, a child! Hours pass... still planning. The man watches for people coming near his house to catch his victim, all night he waits until the next day. The first child walks past at dinner time, slowly he creeps out then follows the child into a dark alley and...

Francesca Lachanudis (11)
South Hunsley School & Sixth Form College, North Ferriby

Red Rum

It was a cold winter's night and Nathan was walking towards a creepy, dark, abandoned mansion. It was coming up to full moon. Right behind Nathan, trees were rustling and howling so Nathan ran into the dark mansion. He hid in a creepy corner and saw a shadow and then the shadow teleported in front of Nathan and said, 'My name is Dylan.' Nathan tried to get out of the haunted mansion but then the doors slammed shut and there was no escape. The ghost got an axe and swung it at Nathan, all you could hear was screaming... silence.

Dylan Williams (11)
South Hunsley School & Sixth Form College, North Ferriby

The Attack!

One afternoon, two boys called Ben and Tom went to the park to play football but soon after it started to get dark so they left to go home. By the time Tom got home, it was very dark. Suddenly, out of nowhere, bullets were being fired. Suddenly, Ben heard Tom scream, 'Help!' Before Ben could run away, sadly, he was shot. Ben's heart was sunk. Sadly, not long after, Ben had been shot. All was silent and that was that.

Lydia Grace Thurston (11)
South Hunsley School & Sixth Form College, North Ferriby

Doll Bones

Josh, woke from a nightmare and the tap, tap, tapping got louder. This hadn't been a dream. How had he ended up in bed? He rushed to the window, and looked out into the garden, a figure appeared, a figure with old-fashioned clothing sat on the grass. He noticed words on his window which said, 'Dare you come to meet me near the apple tree?'
Josh rushed downstairs, slowly walked across the lawn and towards the bottom of the garden. He peered through the dim morning light and suddenly a hand grabbed his shoulder, he yelled...

Georgia Ellis (11)
South Hunsley School & Sixth Form College, North Ferriby

Lakewood

Jake lived in Lakewood, a village on the outskirts of Hull. Just before Halloween, he was invited to a haunted house party but unfortunately he couldn't read properly. Excited by the invite, he turned up a day early, not realising he'd got the wrong day! The house appeared haunted (as Jake expected) and rumour was that the man who lived there, had recently passed away. However, this didn't put Jake off going inside. As Jake opened the door, he heard laughing and saw the shadow of a man flicker across the walls. 'Hello!' called Jake. CCTV captured nothing more...

Samuel Alexander Ogle (11)
South Hunsley School & Sixth Form College, North Ferriby

House Of The Lost

It was a foggy, humid day. James and Alex stumbled upon the house of the lost. Fog circled them as they trekked on the creaky, groaning floorboards, not knowing their fate. Suddenly, James had the outrageous idea to wander off and scare Alex. So he went into the attic. 'James?' Alex shivered. James made his way up to the attic. When Alex followed, he heard distant laughter. Unexpectedly, it stopped. 'James?' Then a scream was heard and James was dragged into the darkness by something. Someone. Never to be seen again. Alex was the next hopeless victim...

Greg Barnabas Longman (14)
South Hunsley School & Sixth Form College, North Ferriby

Dinner Time

Lola sat peacefully playing with her toys. She had waited patiently for over an hour. She gazed towards the ceiling, thinking about everything.
'Lola, your dinner is ready.'
Lola stood up like a bullet, she bashed through her door at an extreme pace. The stairs were in her sight, Lola darted down to the bottom, she passed the living room. All of a sudden, a hand shot out of the basement and pulled her in there!
'Why can I not go in there, Mum?'
'Because I heard the voices come from there too.'

Jack Shanahan (13)
South Hunsley School & Sixth Form College, North Ferriby

The Fall

Tranquillity, peace, that's all there is. Seems a bit too good to be true.
A deer jumping around me, 'I like this,' Jane murmured to herself.
The deer started to talk, 'Jane... Jane, wake up!'
'Did that... thing hit you that hard?'
The two ghosts were in a state of shock. Jessie started with a quivering
voice. Jane got to her feet. The church that they were located in was
the scene of the *Devil Murders*. Suddenly, the door opened.
'Let's find these ghosts.'
They had only a moment to hide.

Lily Lambourne (13)
South Hunsley School & Sixth Form College, North Ferriby

A New Family

It was a standard morning in busy London. The harsh breeze of the
wind whistled through the narrow crack in John's bedroom window.
'8am John, it's time to go.'
A tear rolled down John's face as he was reminded of the day he
would have to go to the country. They arrived at the train station,
greeted by John's fellow classmates.
11am. John's cautiously got off the train where he met his new family.
The man standing before him had a cold stare glancing to the right at
an elderly woman. This wasn't the trip he was hoping for.

Thomas Shirra (13)
South Hunsley School & Sixth Form College, North Ferriby

Chilling Encounter

The Glacier, 23rd January '87
It was cold that day, even for out there. My leg had locked up again,
but Delta Base wasn't too far. I soldiered on, my coat claimed by frost
that desperately clung to it. Recklessly, I hurled it away. Delta Base
wasn't too far. Little did I know, that decision would cost me my life.
It provided no warning. Human, but it wasn't. From the ice, he rose,
pouncing at me like a hungry leopard. With no protection from my
armoured jacket, I plummeted through the ravenous snow.
That's just it.
That's how I died.

Aidan Hannard (13)
South Hunsley School & Sixth Form College, North Ferriby

Insomniac

Night had fallen. The sorrowful moon hung behind ghostly clouds. He
sat there, alone in the dark. Nervously, he peered over his shoulder.
He knew. 15 years ago, he tormented him. He mentally tortured him
into insanity. Regret now filled his mind as he reread the headline
on the newspaper. 'Oh God,' he murmured, petrified. His phone
vibrated. The text read, 'Midnight'. He glanced at the clock. 11:59pm.
Out of the corner of his eye, he caught a glimmer of a sharp tip,
raised in the air. In the room, knife in hand poised to slash, here for
revenge...

Cameron Todd (13)
South Hunsley School & Sixth Form College, North Ferriby

The Creature And Mary

Mary Wicks, a young teenager, slowly looked up at the creature. Was this really happening? Or could she still be dreaming? No... This wasn't a dream, it was a living nightmare. A pair of gloomy, crimson eyes glared at Mary as she lay silently under the covers in her bed. She breathed heavily as the creature's eyes drew through her pinky flesh. She quickly released a yelp and a scream from her tiny mouth that was chattering like an eager train. Hiding under her blankets, trembling with fear, her bold eyes closed as the creature jumped towards her...
'Help!'

Kate Huntington (14)
South Hunsley School & Sixth Form College, North Ferriby

The Psychopath

James sat on his bed on FaceTime with Lily, Lara and Jack. *Slam!* Suddenly, James' window slammed. They were all on about going to town.
James walked up to the window. He looked across at the house opposite; there was a shadow of a man or woman with some type of weapon. *Screech!* It came from that house, which was Lily's...

James Moat (13)
South Hunsley School & Sixth Form College, North Ferriby

The Grave Digger

Raindrops the size of bullets thundered on the church's walls for
days; the walls started crumbling. The flower beds were filled with
black murky water. James went out to meet his friend Sally. They were
meeting at the park. James strolled whilst the bullets still fell on his
head.

James walked past the church's huge doorway. James steadily
glanced at the doors, they were open.

'Sally, is that you?' James cautiously shouted.

James turned around, scanning everywhere. James looked back at
the huge doorway. Sally was dead, with a man stood on top of her
with a shovel.

'You're next!'

Fin Tomlinson (13)
South Hunsley School & Sixth Form College, North Ferriby

Half The World Away

As the metallic helium balloons drifted onto the pallid moon's surface,
a mineral tear fell down Elliott's cheek. Instantly, Elliott opened the
bundle of joy, a colossal beam overcoming his face.

A letter with ruby-red ribbon around it was placed on top of a jet-
black box. He opened it, it read, 'From Earth'. Elliott's hopeful face
expressed a mixture of emotions as he precariously opened the box.
A small, murky cloud overcame Elliott's face when he opened it.
Ashes appeared in front of his face. A mineral tear fell down Elliott's
cheek. The ashes of Alice!

Katy Wells (13)
South Hunsley School & Sixth Form College, North Ferriby

Is This The End?

So... is this the end? It's where I plummet to my death. After everything and now this. I'm on the edge, only a rope holding my life. We lost. I tried to save my people and I failed. I failed everyone. I am alone. All on my own. The days of my ruling are over. I am weak, I have gone astray from my people because my army and myself wasn't strong enough to save anyone.

Who's that? They've come back to get me, is this it? Should I just end this cruel, sad life? No, don't let go!

Cara Portz (13)

South Hunsley School & Sixth Form College, North Ferriby

The Curse Of The Gloomy Lantern

Whilst investigating the death of a local police officer, a brave girl named Clara uncovers a legend about a supernaturally-cursed gloomy lantern circulating throughout Transylvania. As soon as anyone uses the lantern, he or she has exactly 25 days left to live. The doomed few appear to be ordinary people during their day-to-day life, but when photographed, they look skeletal. A marked person feels like a cold dog to touch.

Clara gets hold of the lantern, refusing to believe the superstition. A collage of images flash in her mind: a tired bat balancing on a police officer...

Bex Collier (13)

South Hunsley School & Sixth Form College, North Ferriby

Trapped

Thick, cloudy fog surrounded me and engulfed my every movement. However, in the distance I could see something. Slowly creeping my way forward, I stepped on some old branches that crackled beneath my feet until I came to a large mansion. Most of the ancient, dirty windows were shattered and shards of glass had covered the filthy floor. Creaking, the double doors slithered wide open, welcoming the eerie whistling wind that echoed through the empty building. Taking a few deep and courageous breaths, I tiptoed into the mansion. Suddenly, the doors slammed shut and locked themselves. I was not alone...

Hannah Jackson (14)
South Hunsley School & Sixth Form College, North Ferriby

Murder Manor

'Boo!'
He had failed again. Jeff came up from behind a bin, he looked at me with pain in his eyes. One second, he ran to the Murder Manor. I ran after him, he ran to the garden and I stayed at the door. I looked around, the walls were covered in moss and crumbling. I kept looking over my shoulder in case Jeff tried to scare me. Then I heard a scream.
'Jeff? Jeff, where are you?'
I stood frozen on the spot. I waited and waited until something, or someone, placed a dark, cold hand over my mouth...

Sam Johnson (14)
South Hunsley School & Sixth Form College, North Ferriby

Apparition

As I approached the crumbling graveyard, shadows danced around me. The door creaked open, moonlight shone onto the ancient stained-glass windows. My footsteps echoed... *bang!* I turned in panic, the door had been slammed shut. Approaching footsteps were only metres away from me as cold, howling wind swept past. The room had become unwelcoming, cold shivered down my spine... I jumped at the sound of floorboards creaking. An icy wisp of breath stroked the back of my neck. I swivelled around, a misty cloud coated the floor of the church, an eerie undertone stuck through the haunted building.
'John?'

Jasmine Gregory (13)
South Hunsley School & Sixth Form College, North Ferriby

The Mystery Man

One day, Jimmy and I were walking home. I saw a man, he was trying to hide in the bushes. I whispered to Jimmy, 'Keep to the left.' It was quite a while since we saw the man. We turned the last corner to our house and Jimmy said, 'Is that the same man behind us?' I just said, 'Run!'
We finally got home, we were having a sleepover at mine. We called our parents but they didn't believe us so we went on with it. I woke up that morning and my heart dropped, Jimmy was missing...

Miles Austin Robert Alford (13)
South Hunsley School & Sixth Form College, North Ferriby

The Two Gunshots

On a dark winter's day, two children fought to stay alive. They walked into an old house.

'Hello?' Sarah said with fear.

'Anyone there?' Sudi said with a stammer.

As they both walked in a gunshot went off.

'Sarah!'

As she fell on the floor, tears of blood shot out. Sudi ran to go and get someone. They came, Sarah had gone...

Jacob Mallier, the murderer, buried her in the Yorkshire Moors. Her body was never found but people say Sarah's body is still there now waiting to be found and dug up and brought home to her family...

Blossom Plows (11)
South Hunsley School & Sixth Form College, North Ferriby

The Dead

The girl woke... Everyone was asleep except one... Annabel. She dragged her knife across the path, for the next victim to die. I heard a knock on my door, nobody was there. She's dead, I killed her. Every year it went over again on Friday 13th, midnight. *Bang!* Every dead person, every evil spirit. All came back to kill another. On all their graves was 'Catch 'em, kill 'em!'

Tilly Bell (11)
South Hunsley School & Sixth Form College, North Ferriby

The Disappearing Friend

'You count to 100 Charlie... go!'
I ran into a mansion. Dead roses lay on the ground outside. It looked abandoned. *Slam!* The door shut. A shiver shot down my spine. Inside the creepy house were antiques; some of them looked priceless even though they were covered in dust. I shouted, 'Hello, is anyone at home?' There was no reply. I paused, wondering what to do next. Turning to face the long, dark corridor to my left, I caught sight of a shadowy figure: Charlie!
Suddenly, a voice boomed, 'Get out of my house!'
I never saw little Charlie again.

Annabel Tessier (11)
South Hunsley School & Sixth Form College, North Ferriby

Never Turn Your Back!

Miaow! I woke from my vast sleep. My eyes throbbing with energy; as the feral cats ran over me with fear! But then I wondered, where was I? The clock struck 12am and I knew where I was - I was at the graveyard. I looked behind me, the writing stated, 'In memory of Damon Salvator', and the bold letters said, 'Kill 'em whilst you can'. I thought I was alone... But I heard a loud noise. It was footsteps. Getting louder! I didn't know what to do... I screamed. I felt a cold hand on my shoulder...

Frankie Fields (11)
South Hunsley School & Sixth Form College, North Ferriby

Lurking Darkness

Staggering through the wide hole, no glimpse of light, only darkness surrounding me. I stop to take a rest, knowing I shouldn't. Just as I begin to fall down the side of the wall, I feel a cold gush down my neck, of what I thought was wind... My mind instantly starts to race to conclusions.

'Where are you going?' a hushed voice speaks.

'Home,' I answer quietly.

I can't even hear my own voice.

'Are you sure?'

A dry, bony hand firmly grips my arm, dragging me into the light.

'No! No! Please!' I scream.

But there's no point...

Selina Harlock (12)

South Hunsley School & Sixth Form College, North Ferriby

Is My Cupboard Really Haunted?

I stood there not knowing what to do as I saw my cupboard door open. A hand reached out at me, I screamed a high-pitched C. The hand was cold as ice. I never realised but this time I started screaming for my life. Two minutes later, I heard a knock on the door. The door opened somehow, I was sure I had locked it! A green figure appeared with its hand held in front of it. It was a zombie. I screamed again, not knowing I'd broken two windows already. But then I thought, I was trapped...

Phoebe Buckley (11)

South Hunsley School & Sixth Form College, North Ferriby

The Hotel Of Nightmares

I looked at my watch, then the hotel across the road, then back at my watch. It was too late to travel home now, but there was something not quite right about the hotel. As I stood there getting drenched by the passing storm, I decided to head inside. The doors slammed shut behind me; *it's just the wind,* I reassured myself.
'Hello?' I called out.
'Hello.'
A deep, scary voice came from behind me. I began trembling as I turned around to see a large death-like figure in the corner of the dark, eerie room...

Storm Lambert (14)
South Hunsley School & Sixth Form College, North Ferriby

The Strange House Upon The Hill

There was once an old rusty shack upon a winding hill, as the three brave souls tiptoed up the rocky stairway. They approached the huge door and spotted a shady, black figure out of the corner of their eye. He was watching them. They pushed open the door and stepped in. There was a stone person. As they walked in, it looked like he was trying to escape but he was frozen in stone. A shoe fell down the stairs and screams came from upstairs, they turned to the door to escape. It was locked, they turned...
'Argh!'

Ben Curtis (14)
South Hunsley School & Sixth Form College, North Ferriby

Facing

The street lamp shone in the dark, gloomy street. It flickered vigorously, stopping every once in a while, then starting again. Sat in the familiar living room, the TV chattered away. Suddenly, the TV sparked and popped, switching itself off in the process. The lights dimmed. Outside, the wind howled like a wolf at a full moon. *Bring, bring* went the doorbell. I got up out of my seat and stumbled to the door. I opened it. No one was in sight so I shut the door and faced the living room. Eyes glared at me amongst shadows...

Tom Wharram (13)
South Hunsley School & Sixth Form College, North Ferriby

Behind You!

A shiver ran down Tom's spine as he scanned the room. He carefully stood up and backed up against the wall of crates that he had safely stacked the other day.
'James, is that you?' he called, 'Are you there James? Now's not the time for jokes.'
Suddenly, a hand landed on his shoulder.
'James, is that you?'
Suddenly, from gaps in the crates, the body of James fell next to Tom with a thud. Tom slowly backed up to the window. 'James, are you alright?' he asked in terror. 'What happened to you?'
James started to moan quietly...

Aaron Sleet (13)
South Hunsley School & Sixth Form College, North Ferriby

Then She Was Gone!

In a dark, cold alleyway there was a gloomy, towering house with huge, sharp spikes on top! All of the children were terrified of what was beyond the rusty gates! An adventurous girl in the alleyway liked these sorts of creepy, spooky adventures. One day, she heaved open those creaky gates and stepped inside. Automatically, they closed and she ventured on with nobody close. She wanted to prove herself to the others! She touched the old wooden door and it was suddenly dragged open from the inside. An ancient lady caught hold of her arm. She was never seen again...

Ellie Blood (12)

South Hunsley School & Sixth Form College, North Ferriby

The Curse Of Othalha

It was a dark, stormy night and you were all alone. Your mum and dad had gone out for the night. In your dark, gloomy mansion, there was a blackout and you were lost in the hallways of hell, you felt an evil presence watching you then the next thing you knew you were paralysed in fear and there was a horrible chill running down your spine and it was at that moment you lost it, you were going insane and you couldn't take it anymore and by the time your parents got home, it was too late for you.

Christopher Parkes (11)

South Hunsley School & Sixth Form College, North Ferriby

The Haunted House

I stood still, silent, when the massive brown door screamed as it gave a signal of my presence. Should I enter? As one foot was itching to move forward, the other was saying no! I made my decision. I slowly crept towards the door as it slammed shut. A cold draught of strong wind hit my back and sent a shiver down my spine. I quickly turned to the left then the right, I stopped slowly, turning round, my heart beating one hundred times faster than normal. I stopped, I finally saw it. It was here after all these years...

Mollie Rokahr (13)
South Hunsley School & Sixth Form College, North Ferriby

The Figure

He wakes up in the comfort of his warm bed. He gazes out across the dark room. It's dark but he can just make out the shapes in the area. The TV, computer, shadowy figure, painting, wait... Figure? There it is. Standing in the corner. Motionless. He dashed for the light, gone. No light. Off. There it is. On. Gone. Each time the figure grows closer and closer. He can make out the face now. A man. Suddenly, the man disappears completely. He feels completely safe until he feels a hand on his shoulder.
'This is the end for you... '

Josiah Roy (14)
South Hunsley School & Sixth Form College, North Ferriby

977

The doctors delivered the sad news; cancer had won. Her mother was dead. He started bar hopping; came home one night with a replacement wife. That's when the abuse started. The new wife got in his head.

3 years later, she had had enough; she jumped. The end... or so she'd thought. She found herself in a prison-like, white room, next to a stranger called 976. She was given a name, number, (by her mother, but she'll never know that). She'll be forever beaten for her cowardice, no exceptions even for 12-year-olds. Death doesn't always end it all.

Becky Parkin (12)

South Hunsley School & Sixth Form College, North Ferriby

'Are You In There?'

Footsteps grew louder and louder behind me... we bolted into what once was the church. Hearts pounding, palms sweating, we looked at each other in fright. Panicking, Anna blocked the door with the nearest bookcase. An almost silent knock echoed from the door, as a voice spoke, 'Are you in there?'

The lights flickered on and off, each time we grew further apart until I could no longer see her.

'Anna?'

'She's gone,' the voice whispered.

I backed into a corner, I was all alone. A scream rang around the church. What was or wasn't real?

Ellen Pape (13)

South Hunsley School & Sixth Form College, North Ferriby

The Dead Man

Was he dead? No. He was alive. How could he die? Unless... he was murdered. Which he wasn't, but the blood. Everywhere. Who would murder him? No one would. No one did. It was just a horrible dream. I would wake up soon. Wake up from this nightmare. Although, blood covered my hands. It wasn't a dream. But real. Had I killed him? Maybe I helped? I tried to stop the bleeding. The murderer was another. Surely it wasn't my fault. But the killer's. The person who killed him. He had been killed, he was dead.

Evie Madden (14)
South Hunsley School & Sixth Form College, North Ferriby

Abandoned House

My heart beats violently as I walk cautiously down the passage towards the house. As I open the huge gothic door, it creaks loudly, once I enter I see a flashing lamp and a cracked window. Walking up the gloomy stairway, dust falls onto my sweaty, clammy hands. Reaching the top, suddenly I feel a hand on my back. I hear a bang and loud footsteps from upstairs. I run as fast as my legs can take me down to the door... but it was too late, a figure appeared. *Smash!* Blood seeped out from my body and darkness descended...

Eleanor Morland (13)
South Hunsley School & Sixth Form College, North Ferriby

Everybody's Parents

John was 14 and had a brother, mum and dad. He was always second best and he wanted to run away, but he was faced with an unfair dilemma that was a risk to his life. His family wasn't who he thought they were. He was targeted the whole time and his real family was dead. He was in fact about to be changed forever, as his family had implanted something into his brain. His family wasn't human and he was locked inside himself forever. No one knows how or why it happened but these people are still out there.

George William Henry Bidder (13)
South Hunsley School & Sixth Form College, North Ferriby

Down-Town Pond

One night after dark, five kids thought it would be fun to play some games in the creaky forest next to Down-Town pond. They started to play a game of hide-and-seek so they decided to make some eerie noises to creep the seeker out. After a while, the seeker got scared and went home, so did the other two, until it was only Ben and Craig left. When he was seeking, Craig was shouting, 'Ben! Ben!' There was no reply. As Craig was shuffling backwards, he didn't notice the black waters of the pond...
There were only ripples...

Joe Mitchell (11)
South Hunsley School & Sixth Form College, North Ferriby

Bloodsuckers Like It Fresh

Life is short and then you die. Unfortunately, I'm not dead. My eyes flicker open. Silence. I can't move. Claustrophobia seeps into my brain, making me sick. Dank walls grip me, constricting my arms and legs from large movement. Questions explode in my mind. I'm trapped in a coffin. Fear overwhelms me. My heart hammers against my chest. I kick hopelessly at the side of the sarcophagus, hoping for it to give way. The oxygen slowly begins to evacuate. A faint scratching echoes behind my ears; the horrifying sound of desperate fingernails scraping above my head. I'm not alone.

Polly Crawley (14)
Upper Wharfedale School, Skipton

November Nights

Fluffy, soft quill dancing on the piece of paper as I write about my horror. As rain hits the window and the candle flame flickers in the room, it will not stop. The noise. Everything I've done to stop it has not prevailed. It will not stop. The eerie sound gets closer every day. No matter what I do, no matter how hard I try, it perseveres. It won't stop. Yesterday, I seized hold of the kitchen knife and hacked at my ears. I can't hear anything now. Just that noise as it taps on through the crisp, November nights.

Jake Price (15)
Upper Wharfedale School, Skipton

Hospital Horror

Lily's body oozed with a ruby-red thin liquid. I peered outside at the windy revolting weather. So many questions ran through my mind, how did I get here? Why's Lily dead?

I slowly made my way onto the ancient, daunting corridor. I could hear the vulgar assassin lurking near. Suddenly, I could feel his warm, putrid breath on my neck. It was too late to run! An excruciating pain ran throughout my entire body, I fell to the ground reaching for the weapon. Slowly, I turned to watch my murderer laughing as I took my last breath.

Emily Howarth

Upper Wharfedale School, Skipton

Who's Got Millie?

Millie had been missing for three miserable years now. She constantly felt the cool, crisp air cutting through her. She was lonely. All she wished for was to be found, to have someone.

One particular evening, she was trudging through the damp, dense forest, the wind screaming above her. She kept going as she always did, through night-time rustles. Everything she'd heard before. When the noises carried on, Millie's heart raced like never before. 'Hello?' she stuttered. Nothing.

Suddenly, a bloodless, icy hand fell on her shoulder. 'So Millie, your wishes came true, I've found you, you've got me now... '

Lucy Harford (14)

Upper Wharfedale School, Skipton

Where Is She?

Winter was here again. One depressing night, Josie and I went into Whitby for the longest walk ever. There was someone following us I swear, but Josie said otherwise. She told me to calm down. My mind wouldn't let me, I was panicking. When we got to the bottom of the 199 steps, Josie said we should count them, to calm me down. We got halfway, a rock flew past my head. There was something following us. I was right! All I could see was a black-as-night figure. It ran towards me, said, 'Shhh!' and grabbed Josie...

Emma Noble (14)
Upper Wharfedale School, Skipton

No Escape

Death has come to Woodsborough. There is no escape, no freedom. All that I can do is embrace my fate. Death is patient, mercilessly stalking the helpless prey that is myself. As I take refuge in the still, silent graveyard, I feel my heart beat like a drum as I begin to hyperventilate. The wind howls and the moon casts its eerie glare on me as I huddle into a foetal position. Then I begin to hear an eerie, unnatural outcry behind me. My life seems to flash before my eyes. This must be it. Death has come for me...

Alfie Page (14)
Upper Wharfedale School, Skipton

Not About A Cat!

An eerie silence swept through the ghostly cellar. It was murky. As black as coal. Rats scurried around the floor looking into barrels and crops, searching for food. Blood-curdling creaks pierced my ears. Then suddenly, out of the sooty eventide, leapt a clown baby doll. Bloodthirsty eyes stared into my soul as I backed gingerly into the red-brick wall that lurked just behind me. Wet saliva drooled from its gaping mouth, as the sharp, pointy, vampire teeth crept towards me. Witch-like make-up made the dead of night increasingly more graphic. What was to come?

James Mukherjee (13)
Upper Wharfedale School, Skipton

Death At Night

In the dead of night, I was running with my friends who thought it was a good idea to visit the ancient forest at eventide, November; I said I would join them on this blood-curdling twilight. It began to rain so we took refuge in the closest building, which was an eerie, decrepit church. I didn't mind. I overheard the two others saying they heard a scream, neither wanted to go look. One finally went to check. *Bang.* He hit the ground. I found my other friend, they screamed as I got closer; I grabbed their necks then dead silence...

Harvey Holme (13)
Upper Wharfedale School, Skipton

The Eerie Farm

Misty, eerie Halloween dusk. We're at a creepy, decrepit farm. We go to the door, as soon as we knock, blood starts pouring out from under the door. We start to walk away when a big, tall man comes out with fangs. There is a heart in one hand and the other is covered in blood. It looks like we're his next victims. We run but he catches us, one by one. Stops for a few seconds, then rips the others' hearts out. The trees are moving like they're alive in the wind. I get cornered and he comes. Nearer...

Oliver Hruby-Horn (13)
Upper Wharfedale School, Skipton

Claw Bloodbath

Lights went off. Humans screamed. Black smoke rose outside the decrepit window. My target tiptoed across the intimidating hallway, with exhausted candles down either side. Leaping like a tiger attacking its prey, landing directly onto my target. I dug my teeth into the veins on the side of the neck, blood poured out onto the eerie floor. The sounds of rats lurking around, waiting to eat what's left over when I'm gone. My long abnormal claws ripped open the chest of the human, the heart popped out along with lungs and lots of blood. I was in a bloodbath.

Abbie Kellow (13)
Upper Wharfedale School, Skipton

The Barn

An inky mist rolls in. Before me is a great, exhausted stone barn. Midnight approaches. I'm tired and frozen. Forward I go through the murky mist. This place is extremely unnerving, the barn is getting no closer. Suddenly, rain starts to hammer down, colder, colder. Must get to the barn. Above me looms the ancient barn, safety. Breaking through the gloomy mist, I stumble into the barn. On the floor in front of me is an axe. An axe with blood. From behind me, comes an unearthly smell. All of a sudden, the barn has become like hell.

Charlie Theodosius (13)
Upper Wharfedale School, Skipton

The Unwanted

Stacy was walking in the dead of night. Alone, she found herself lost, not knowing which direction to go in. Clouds of fog gathered above her, suddenly there was a snap, then three gigantic bangs. She wondered if someone was trying to warn her. As she glanced up, squinting through the fog, Stacy saw a massive red and yellow tent. She crept closer, almost touching the tent door. Her eye peered through like a bullet leaving a gun. A small puff let out over her shoulder, she slowly turned, not wanting to upset the creature. Blood trickled down his chin...

Bradie Dean (14)
Upper Wharfedale School, Skipton

The Dolls Are Alive

Looking around the eerie room, I huddle underneath the sheets. Terrified. Dolls glare at me from shelves, bookcases and cupboards. Grandma has this strange obsession of collecting dolls, it is blood-curdling.

I hear a sound, a girl singing, I turn my head towards the noise, finding myself face-to-face with a doll. Trying to take it in, I'm too stunned to scream. Looking down, big mistake. I find that there are now dolls on my bed. They stare at me like tigers homing in to kill. Next thing I see, she has a knife in her cold, porcelain hand...

Mollie Ward (13)
Upper Wharfedale School, Skipton

The Eerie Castle

Mist cascaded over the ominous castle. I walked towards the metal door - it flung open. Walking in, I could hear a murmur. The door banged shut behind me. I was all alone. To the left of me was a doll. I picked her up and placed her onto the rocking chair. I heard talking. She was gone. It was like all the life had been taken. I ran back to the door, trying to open it. My hands were as cold as ice. I could not open the door so I smashed a window. I was too late.

Hattie Watkinson (13)
Upper Wharfedale School, Skipton

The Beckoning Building

Night fell on the eerie castle in the distance. The remains lying mysteriously ahead of me. Inky black shadows haunted the ghostly castle. Flashbacks were racing through my head from this chilling moment in time, two years ago. Screams. Cries. Screeches. Cackles of old women beckoned me. Cries of children, deathly voices threatening me. The spine-chilling shadows lurked on the ancient walls of the creepy building. The foggy air sent a shiver down my spine as something tapped me on the shoulder. Whispers struck at the dead of night. Screeches deafened me, as I got closer and closer...

Chloe Metcalfe (13)

Upper Wharfedale School, Skipton

Run Away

Running away was intimidating, especially at twilight. The blood-curdling forest is where I ran to. The forest was decrepit and didn't seem friendly. A cave was my habitat for the night. I rested my head on a rock in the belly of the cave. I was facing the entrance. Suddenly, a silhouette appeared at the mouth of the cave. It wandered towards me slowly. It was wearing a ball gown and top hat. It ran to me. I got up. It grabbed me in its clutches. It hit me on the head, I woke up in a darkened basement...

Sonny Meldon (13)

Upper Wharfedale School, Skipton

The Uninvited Visitor

On an ominous, gloomy twilight, I could just see the outline of a mysterious building through the gloom. I stood at the entrance of what used to be Bran Castle, slaughter house, I could hear the crows alarming me to turn away. As I entered, I was intimidated by the bloodstained tools and pools of blood below.
I ventured onwards into the mysterious unknown. I felt everywhere I went there was a presence following me like a shadow. I made my way down a staircase. Under the slaughter house was a figure standing there, looking towards me, waiting...

Max Marsden (13)
Upper Wharfedale School, Skipton

The Figure

Midnight struck, her eyes were menacing. The alarming atmosphere surrounding them. Amy screamed for help, the ominous figure quickly glued her unnerving hand over Amy's mouth, muffling her screams. The possessed, unearthly creature had murky, unbearable hair ragged up into pigtails. Her long, rotting nails pushed through Amy's chest, her last whiff of obscure air was filled with the polluted atmosphere and the weakened perfume from the blood-curdling creature. Amy's legs slowly fell. Blood was pouring out like a fallen wine bottle. Everywhere was quiet. The unwanted creature walked away, leaving the innocent corpse to rot.

Caitlin Ambler (14)
Upper Wharfedale School, Skipton

Should I Turn?

Standing in the abandoned fairground, intensely frosty and sodden. Walking around trying to perceive where I was, in the witching hour. Trying to identify anything. I heard noises in the distance. Scavenging around, I suddenly bumped into something, all I could see was a glistening red ball. As the light flickered I was trying to glance and peer up like a meerkat. Suddenly, it vanished. Turning around whilst soiling myself, there it was, a blood-curdling clown with a deformed eye that didn't move an inch.

'Turn around young boy and prepare,' it slowly and quietly said. 'Right now, this second.'

George Hayton (14)
Upper Wharfedale School, Skipton

Twitching Silhouette

Once stepped upon, the brittle planks of the deserted hallway, a creak snapped within the unnerving atmosphere. The thundering of my heart was all I dared to hear as it boomed in my ears. Each glaring rag of curtain kept still. Too still. I continued as all I could see was the light of the bitter full moon. A piercing screech echoed through the hallway as a frail figure passed the edge of my vision. My heart was wracking my body. A woman, twitching body, black eyes came forward. Twitching... just twitching! She grinned. Everything became black. Help me... Please!

Ella Bentley (15)
Upper Wharfedale School, Skipton

First The Left, Then The Right

During the shadowy duskiness of 31st October, I decided to set off to terrify the young blonde at number one. I put together a plan. Approaching an open window leading to the kitchen of house number one, I hauled my body through it. I was in! Excitedly, I waited patiently. As soon as she approached the kitchen, I took a shot. Gouging out her left eyeball, then her right. It felt as normal as walking does. After her eyes were gone, I sucked every ounce of blood left in her fragile body. My first victim's gone. But who's my next?

Amanda Brown (14)
Upper Wharfedale School, Skipton

The Disappearance

A gloomy fog surrounded the ship. I was alone. Everyone was gone. The blackness of the midnight sky was ghostly. It was as black as space. All the passengers were gone except me. I looked around the inky, gloomy ship, to find someone. There was no life.
Suddenly, I heard a noise. I ran across the lifeless ship to find someone. A young man was staring into the unearthly sea. He turned around and stared into my soul. He had a knife. Suddenly, the blade went through his mouth and blood dripped down the bloody knife. I was alone.

Sam Newey
Upper Wharfedale School, Skipton

Working Late

Slowly, I walk down the creaky stairs. I notice a suspicious letter. So I cautiously grab it. 'Please come to the hospital as soon as you can to help a patient in room 74', it reads. I quickly rush through the door and into the pitch-black world. Once in my car, I rush towards the outside of town. Finally, I approach the building, as the trees surrounding me are like giants watching over me. I enter the silent hospital. As I walk into room 74, I see blood everywhere. I run out and stare down the corridor in fear...

Calum Naylor (13)
Upper Wharfedale School, Skipton

The Ripper

My car started to smoke. I had to pull over. The torch in the boot had no batteries. The next town was a few miles away. Looking down at the road, I saw an ominous orange glow. I turned. There was a cloud that was beating strangely, like a heart. It dissipated. A wooden chair was left. Immediately, I ran, but a ghostly figure floated before me. I tripped up trying to run. My blood curdled and a shiver shuddered through my body. The last thing I saw was the shadowy, ghostly figure looming over me, I fainted...

Jack Barugh (14)
Upper Wharfedale School, Skipton

I Saw Him In The Mirror!

I needed to get away... I was wandering in the damp, lonely woods. *Crash, bang!* I went tumbling down the hill. I found myself at the feet of a hulking, black gate, towering over me. As the gate swung open, I saw a derelict school. Five delicate steps towards the school, I jumped as the door flew open. As I stepped in, the door slammed shut behind me. An ancient cracked mirror hung in the corner of the room, footsteps coming towards me. A loud voice appeared, 'I'm coming for you!' I turned, he was in the mirror.
'Hello?'

Alys Janssen (13)
Upper Wharfedale School, Skipton

Ghostly Figures

I was lost in a forest on a starless night. I saw an old, decaying house. It didn't look that inviting, but it was better than nothing. Slowly, I approached. When I got in, I looked for somewhere to sleep. I saw an ancient chair inches thick with dust. When I had swept the chair down, I began to feel sleepy and took a seat. Eventually, I got some sleep. I woke up to a bang upstairs, so I went to investigate. It was there. A ghostly figure was there! I screeched, calling for help, nobody came...

George Lewis Arkwright (12)
Upper Wharfedale School, Skipton

The Swamp

The fog in the swamp slowly crept in, infecting everything it touched. As I walked, an old, white church came into view. When I got closer, I could see the ancient tombstones leaning and crumbling. The doors creaked and groaned as I pushed them open. Everything was perfectly normal; the flames on the ornate purple candles flickered. I looked and saw a girl, no more than five, stood at the altar in a soaking wet, white robe, her black hair swayed viciously with the wind. She turned her head, opened her eyes and the candles went out like a light...

Rossi Kilburn (14)
Upper Wharfedale School, Skipton

The House Of Shudders!

It was cold, wet and damp. Nobody to be seen. The rain pounded down against the solid path, bouncing off the wall. Lightning and thunder struck - typical British weather. I had to reassure myself. The rain got heavier. The wind howled like a wolf. Nervous, I kept on walking. I opened the rusty brown front door. 'Aunty Maria?' I called. 'Aunty Maria?' No sound. I looked round the corner... nothing to be seen. The floorboards creaked. I jumped. My heart was racing so fast. Something touched me.
'Aunty Maria, is that you?'

Ava Chisnall (12)
Upper Wharfedale School, Skipton

Hunted Man

It's dark and raining. My gang decides to go to the building right in front of us. The further I walk, the more I fear broken gravestones, glass on the floor.

'Argh. What was that?'

As I look up, glass comes pouring down as I see crows pouring down.

'Quick, into the church.'

As we walk around the house, a shadow follows. Doors start creaking, voices start, a man comes out of the door. We run, the man comes, saying, 'Stop!'

He starts running at this point, we are running for our lives, we never made sounds again.

Joshua Ling (13)
Upper Wharfedale School, Skipton

The Haunting

I keep looking back as the car keeps following me. I check behind, making sure he's not looking for anyone, I stop to see if the car will go past, it stops. I look inside, there is no one there. I stick my hand through the open window, I just feel a breeze. I carry on walking, the engine of the car starts again. I decided to investigate. A face pops up, screaming in my face. I get pulled into the car. Dead children everywhere, including me.

Charlotte Barrett (12)
Upper Wharfedale School, Skipton

The Clearing

Walking through the forest with the misty, gloomy darkness crawling slowly upon us, we knew we had to set up camp. As we walked along, we bumped into an ancient clearing and set up our tents, 'I think we should call home,' exclaimed Andrew.
Jim replied, 'Did you just hear that?'
Suddenly, there was a loud shriek coming from the well in the middle of the clearing. Jim and Andrew both looked over the well...
Then Jim's head was ripped off his shoulders. As Andrew started to run away in fear, a skull was thrown at his head. *Bang!* Dead.

Henry Ellison (12)
Upper Wharfedale School, Skipton

The Voice In The Woods

The wind blew upon me as I looked for my brother, As I walked into the forest, I felt someone was watching me. The trees were hands reaching out for freedom from the forest, the fog caged me and I couldn't see where I was. I thought I saw someone but when I looked again, they were gone. I heard a giggle from deeper in. I screamed at the top of my lungs, 'Where are you?'
Yet another giggle was heard, so I shouted, 'You're not my brother, are you?'
Then a voice shouted, 'I am your nightmare.'

Jeremiah Newton (13)
Upper Wharfedale School, Skipton

The Chilly Creeps

The rain is dropping down on the ground as hard as bullets. Swaying side to side, I can't see ahead of me because of all the mist and fog. I enter the castle with a chill running through my spine. I take a look and the first impression is old and creepy. I see a chair with the paperwork I have to do. I sit down, I hear a thud. I look around, no one there. I hear it again, no one there. I think to myself, *what could that be?* I go to have a look and stop. *Bang!*

Toby James Webster (12)
Upper Wharfedale School, Skipton

The Tale Of The Black Dog

Whoosh! went the wind, on the night that transformed my life! I was on top of the rolling hill of Bungay, viewing a vast, picturesque landscape. The landscape stared at me. Such a seductive sight to see, before I transcended my humanity! I was assimilating the pure beauty that the landscape had to offer. I heard it! The hellish howl of a black dog. Except, this wasn't any ordinary black animal. It was a supernatural apparition. It had glowing red, malevolent eyes. It had bared teeth. It had a silvery pelt. And it changed me; my humanity was lost forever!

Adnan Chowdhury (15)
Upper Wharfedale School, Skipton

Wink Murder

'Anyone wanna play a game?'

'Let's play wink murder.'

Kevin, Lisa, Michelle and Sarah were all sat in a circle.

'Right, everyone close your eyes.'

All foggy in the cellar, nobody could see anything but then... Michelle slightly opened her eyes, there was something ghostly there so she just closed them. 'Raaaa!'

'Right everyone, open your eyes.'

'Sarah? Sarah?'

Sarah was lying on the floor, not making any noise, she was frozen. Pitch-black silence... something was there lurking around them. The door slammed. *Bang!*

Lisa screeched, 'Help, somebody.'

'Lisa, are you there?'

'Yes, I'm here.'

Bang!

'Hello? Hello!'

Beth Allwood

Upper Wharfedale School, Skipton

Anastacia

My face was as white as the moon, as if I'd been drained of life. Anastacia stood in front of me. She warned me, exclaiming how I killed her but she was back. Pacing down the ward I realised this was the end. All alone, I sat in the heart of the hospital in horror and dread. Silently, I waited for the impossible. Screaming for help, lights started to blink. Anastacia was playing with my head, one moment there, another moment here. She stabbed a knife into my heart. Now I'm dead but, she will wish she never killed me.

Chloe Winter (14)
Upper Wharfedale School, Skipton

The Woodsman

The house was a dark shadow on the hill. Theo and Clark were exploring the woods when they found it. The boys moved up to the decaying stone door. Clark turned the doorknob. The door opened and the boys saw the silver figure of the murderous woodsman who had lived there previously. Clark was the only one with brains. Theo, however, had none. The ghost was upon Theo as fast as lightning. The ghost raised an axe. *Slam!* The axe fell down on Theo's neck. His windpipe dropped out. Blood was everywhere. Theo was dead. Collapsing, Clark died alone. Gone.

Sam McCartan (13)
Upper Wharfedale School, Skipton

Truth Or Dare?

'Truth or dare?' Tim said to his friend, whilst stood in the ancient graveyard.
'Dare,' Harry replied with a tremble in his voice.
'I dare you to run into the church.'
'OK,' Harry replied.
He walked slowly through the overgrown grass to an old, heavy wooden door. He opened the door, walked into a web-packed, historic church. *Slam!* The door shut. Harry screamed. Tim ran through the overgrown grass, cutting his legs. He got to the door.
'Harry, it's alright, open the door!'
Tim heard a rustle in the bushes, maybe it was safer in the church...

Annabel Clarke (13)
Upper Wharfedale School, Skipton

Anrol

Anrol fled down the abandoned street. All black, the Range Rover growled, as I drove the beast to the deserted warehouse. Standing isolated in an empty warehouse was an abhorrent feeling, but I would not be alone for long. Time passed gradually as I sat waiting for Anrol. *Bang*. With that, the door crashed to the floor. Anrol stood. Red liquid oozing out of his skull. Walking towards him, I took the knife out of my pocket. Teasing him, I moved the knife around the throat, cutting him slightly with one swift movement, I stabbed him in the throat.

Joseph Tiplady (14)
Upper Wharfedale School, Skipton

The Clown That Couldn't Wait For Lunch

Standing inside a desert like swimming pool in the ex-water park, I find myself searching for the dog I've stalked from the town. Suddenly, it appeared at the edge of the pool like it had just blinked into the scene. Chains clanking all around me like an atmosphere just as the beast began to limp. With every step, the dog turned from clown then back to dog. The chains clanked. Eyes fixed on the figure. Suddenly, the dog disappeared leaving only the clown and leaving me chained up, again, alone. The clown is now limping towards me, looking hungry...

William Wade (14)
Upper Wharfedale School, Skipton

Untitled

What was that noise? Dan, are you there? What is this place? It was shady and depressing, I was too frightened to walk any closer. *Bang! What was that?*
'Dan, if you can hear me, come to the door!'
How can one game of hide-and-seek turn out like this?
'Dan, this isn't funny anymore! Stop playing around.'
I turned around slowly, and there it was, a black figure staring, behind the rusty, ancient house. I knew that it wasn't Dan. I closed my eyes and said to myself, *this isn't real, this isn't real.* I opened my eyes...

Kirsty Lister (13)
Upper Wharfedale School, Skipton

Mortem Patris Mei (The Death Of My Father)

A man, a man unlike any other. Simultaneously strong but ethereal. You can never escape him, only evade him momentarily. He moves like the shadows clinging to the darkness despite being as solid as the earth beneath you. No teeth, but could tear you apart raw. Appearing defenceless, but as tough as an army. Never without work. The evidence is stacked against him but he's never found guilty. Your worst nightmare. The bringer of death. These were the last words of my father. By dawn, he was a disembowelled corpse with half his stomach gone. The death bringer had come.

Christopher Heseltine (14)
Upper Wharfedale School, Skipton

The House On The Marsh

As I looked up at the house, I felt a shiver travel down my back. It felt larger in real life than on the picture in the museum. It's said a lady once lived here many moons ago and no one knows what happened to her. It's been abandoned ever since.

My hand trembled with fear as I held the handle to open it. It slowly creaked open, my heart beating like mad. It opened to an extensive kitchen; everything was laid out as though a meal was about to be prepared. The door slammed shut. That's when I knew.

Natasha Rose Elsworth (13)
Upper Wharfedale School, Skipton

Big Jake Is Back

I am now lost because of Josh and his bad directions but I see a church up ahead, I could sleep there and call Josh in the morning. I look inside, looks nice apart from that broken window. I settle down for the night, then there's a voice.
I shout, 'Who's there?'
They reply, 'It's Big Jake. I was coming to get you!'
'I am not the person you want really!'
A shadow appears then, a very large creature.
'Don't hurt me Big Jake.'
'I won't, ha, ha, ha!'
They were the last words I ever heard.

Jack Shaw (12)
Upper Wharfedale School, Skipton

No Going Back

Emily's hand jolted forward, a firm grip grasped her.
Susan whispered, 'It's not too late to turn back.'
Without hesitating, she pushed the creaking door.
'Hello?' she beckoned. She shuffled forward. *Bang!* The girls screamed.
'It's only the door!' said Emily. 'You can let go of my hand.'
As she looked down at her hand, she saw a crippled blood-dripping hand. She fled, jumping all the time, not stopping, not knowing if it was still behind her. She looked over her shoulder. *Crash.* She'd run into something. She looked up to see Susan's dead, lifeless body.

Ben Riley (13)
Upper Wharfedale School, Skipton

The Hidden

Nothing to be seen. Mist everywhere.
'I knew this was a bad idea.'
I walk 100 steps forwards, binoculars just sitting there. I pick them up, look into them. I can't see anything, only mist. I look closer, I see a barn, there's a sign that says *Secret Entrance*. I feel a cold breeze on my neck.
'Joe, is that you?'
A cold voice says, 'Run, boy.'
I look behind me, a black figure. I run for my life. I see the barn, not thinking, I go straight inside. A body falls off the window.
'No, Joe!'
'It's always me.'

Archie Wain (13)
Upper Wharfedale School, Skipton

Creepy Forest

There I was standing in an immeasurable forest. I was creeped out by the fact it was pitch-black and showering with rain. I started running down the path, hearing little sniggers from a little girl that was nowhere to be seen. The trees were waving goodbye. I saw another big shadow other than mine facing me, it was like a ghost or demon or something like that. I ran for my life, scared to death. I heard a massive *bang!* like a gunshot and fell to the floor. It was cold and I was scared to death!

Jack Duggan (12)
Upper Wharfedale School, Skipton

The See-Through Ghost

'Why do we have to be here Shelly?'
There are sharp, pointy spikes everywhere and gravestones in the yard of the eerie haunted house. It's the spookiest place I have ever been in; there are cobwebs everywhere, lights flickering and candles floating. The lights went out, blood was oozing down the walls. Then we saw it, it was a... Argh, Shelly screamed. She disappeared. She had vanished, all that was left was her vibrant light green rucksack. I went upstairs looking for my sister when the door closed really firmly behind me and the see-through ghost appeared...

Emily Skelton (13)
Upper Wharfedale School, Skipton

The Nursing Home Predator

Screeches of laughter split the bitter air surrounding the decrepit nursing home. The voice was calm, yet unnerving. Twisting the rotting door handle, squeals of pain ongoing, I entered the deathtrap. Hesitating, I thought for a moment that the woman had vanished. The night was as still as sleeping crows. I turned cautiously. There it was. A sight of lifeless pensioners, spread across the corridor, a nightmare in itself. She stood there smiling uncontrollably. Purposefully creeping towards me, she had a crazed look in her eyes. My legs were useless. She was death closing in and I was her prey...

Kieran Barker (15)
Upper Wharfedale School, Skipton

The HMS Downfall

'It's too foggy Captain, we're not going to get to London.'
'Just keep going, we'll make it.'
Bang!
'Captain, we've hit something on the port side, we're leaking water, we've got to stop it from reaching the engine room.'
Bang!
'Captain, we have no power, we're shark meat!'
Eventually, the ship swayed side to side and eventually hit something that stopped them in their tracks. The crew shone lights at the mysterious object and one of the crew shouted, 'It's a battleship from the war.'
'Captain, look it's a tidal wave.'
'Look out... '

Harry Clifford Gaskell (13)
Upper Wharfedale School, Skipton

Psycho Prison

I walked into the dark, gloomy prison, curiously looking around. I could see writing engraved into the wall. There was a window wide open with a shadowy figure of a tree that looked like it was going to scratch along the junky filthy floor in the distance. There was a shadowy figure. I sprinted off while I heard a loud chuckle. I hid in a cupboard. Then he smashed the doors off and put a knife to my neck. There was another figure behind him. He crept forward and put out a rotted hand on his shoulder, then shrieked...

Nathan Leigh (13)
Upper Wharfedale School, Skipton

Release The Clowns

Nightfall is the most ominous, ghostly part of the evening. I was pacing through the treacherous forest when I came across an abandoned mineshaft, it looked decent enough for me to spend the witching hour in, so I went to investigate. After wandering the depths of this blood-curdling cave, I discovered bloodstains streaked along the walls. In the distance, there were heavy footsteps approaching me, I squinted to look deeper and saw a bloodied up clown holding an axe, therefore I immediately sprinted in the other direction to find another messed-up clown awaiting my presence...

Nicole Coleman (13)
Upper Wharfedale School, Skipton

On The Run

Gloomy, dim and shadowy, a typical cold winter's twilight. My wristwatch strikes 12:15am, let the witching hour begin. Glancing up at the skyline, an intimidating, blood-curdling castle awaits its next customer. Who's next? The ancient path that lies beneath me seems to go on forever. Ominous woods surround me and the inky fog lays heavy around. Carrying on walking, my torch all of a sudden goes out! Oh no! A cold, wet hand grabs my shoulder. Another hand grabs my leg. Letting out a scream, my mouth gets covered up. They pull me to the floor. What's happening next?

Lucy Whyte (14)
Upper Wharfedale School, Skipton

The Possessed One!

Trying to escape the lurking shadow that emerged from beyond the mist, not knowing what the mysterious creature was, I darted across the woodland as fast as a rampaging bull - within a split second I plunged into a chasm. Scrambling helplessly, trying to clutch onto hope. Wishing this nightmare would come to an end. Grasping for dear life. The thrashing came to a halt. Suddenly, I woke up to hear knocking on glass. At first, I thought it was the window until I heard it come from the mirror again - I looked to see my reflection blink... Boo!

Siyam Ali (15)
Upper Wharfedale School, Skipton

The Myth Of The Lost City

I was running for my life because the myth of the lost city was chasing me. The myth was true, it's not a myth. Trust me, it's not a myth. I turned a corner and started to run, but when I got close to the stairway, it seemed to shrink and get further away. I stopped and something very large and slimy, a monstrous thing sliced and scraped at my ankles. I fell to the floor in pain. It grabbed me by the ankles and picked me up. My scream was the last thing I ever heard.

Jacob Gregson (12)
Upper Wharfedale School, Skipton

Shipwrecked

It was here it all began. We were shipwrecked. Beginning a tale of sorrow, pain and torture, My name is Jack and I'm with Jacob.
'Hello,' said Jacob.
Swish...
'Did you hear that?' I trembled, my face pale with fright. Jacob made a joke and we both laughed. 'Ninjas don't exist Jacob!' I shouted, still laughing.
The smile was wiped off my face when I saw the Joshin's samurai on patrol. I reacted too late, the samurai were onto us, the last thing we saw was a flash of steel as the kissaki pierced someone's flesh and...

Jack Cooper (12)
Upper Wharfedale School, Skipton

Whispers!

'Hello!'
Sarah's breath was heavy from running. She was lost, she knew that now. The stars were unseen and there was an unidentified presence as the fog danced among the trees like lost spirits. Sarah crept closer to the lifeless trees. A bird sat upon the lonely branches, the trees were begging for the moonlight to reach them through the fog. Sarah heard a whisper from deep in the woods, she edged closer and saw an abandoned hut standing among the trees, like it owned them. The whispers got closer, louder, she recognised that they were screaming, 'Kill, kill, kill!'

Michelle Walker (12)
Upper Wharfedale School, Skipton

Trapped

'Why can't this car start?'

'I don't know, but we can't stand out here in the rain so let's go into that house for the night.'

The house looked abandoned, there were twenty rotten graves at the front of the house, the gate had spikes on it, also there was dry blood on the spikes. The sky was black as space, the rain felt heavy, around the place smelt like drains.

'We can't sleep there for the night.'

'We have to because we could freeze to death.'

'Look this isn't that bad.'

'Guess so, but David, are you touching me?'

Adam Pearson (13)

Upper Wharfedale School, Skipton

The Wrong Turn

It is a dark, gloomy night and I have to get to Phill's party. This is the quickest way I know. The fog's really creeping in. I start to look around, I'm just scaring myself, I keep thinking that, until I see a murky figure at the end of the path. Suddenly, a colossal crack of thunder, I look up as it starts to drizzle, I look back at the figure. It's gone! I start sprinting my way. This is a lot longer than I remember, it doesn't seem to stop. I feel over the roots and the misty figure...

Sam Walker (12)

Upper Wharfedale School, Skipton

Dog Walk

I am walking my dog just like always when I hear a chainsaw. There are no trees for miles, so I run. I turn back, I can see a ghostly figure running behind me. What do I do? It's a dead end, I throw my dog over the wall and climb over, I turn around to see where this thing is and see a blade of a chainsaw. I run but I don't know how to get home, so I run into the woods. But then I can hear more voices. What do I do? I am trapped.

Henry Reynard (13)
Upper Wharfedale School, Skipton

A Short Winter

Soaked in the blood of my family, I thought I was the only one left. The heavy snow blocked me in. It was numbing. I could see my breath.
I ran into the cellar, my father after me. I quickly locked the door. My father slammed the cellar windows, smashing them. He hungered for my flesh, there was no way to escape him. His overalls dripped blood on me. At this moment, I thought that I would suffer the same fate as my mother who was being digested in his stomach. I was ready to die...

Harry Simpson (12)
Upper Wharfedale School, Skipton

Midnight's Evil

I was in a misty graveyard at 12 at night. I couldn't find my way home because my sense of direction in the dark is atrocious. I saw a house through the mist but it was the only thing I could see. I walked past all the crumbling, indecipherable gravestones right up until I was against it. I opened the door and walked through. It slammed behind me. I slowly turned round, trying not to imagine what it could be. When I turned, there it was, looming over me...

Sam Foster (12)
Upper Wharfedale School, Skipton

The Flash

I wondered how long I had been listlessly wandering. A day, two days, maybe even a week, knowing how time went differently in this dreaded labyrinth. Next time the king wants someone to find *the lost*, he can jolly well do it himself.
Suddenly, I was pulled away from my thoughts as I noticed a head, on a platter, his face twisted in agony. I saw thirteen of these heads, their faces all the same way.
I stopped. There was one more platter, with my name on it. I heard a click. Someone had turned out all the lights...

Fergus Cooper (12)
Upper Wharfedale School, Skipton

The Spine-Chiller

The car engine sounded like a popcorn machine as it came to a stop. The skies rumbled like a thunderstorm as a thick, misty fog rolled in from the horizon. The scene was eerie with gravestones and an abandoned cemetery. I got out and saw a cross with a faint glow. 'This place is spooky,' I cried.
I shouted out loud after I fell into an open grave. I felt and could touch the mud when I landed. Before I fell, I read the name on the gravestone above the open grave. And it said my name, *Jack Barton.*

Milosz Butowski (13)
Upper Wharfedale School, Skipton

The Temptation

'Hello?'
My voice echoed around the decrepit house darting onto every wall, then eventually coming back to me. It was dark outside; dense mist surrounded the house like it was in its own world. Every move crows squeaked and bats fluttered away. I knew I shouldn't be here but it was somehow enticing. I carried on into the depths of the house, soon realising that no one lived here. Coldness crept up my spine, fear raced into my head. Feeling the intimidating presence of somebody, I turned around. After that, my memory gets hazy…

Alex Patrick Birtley (14)
Upper Wharfedale School, Skipton

The Woman In The Forest

Explosion of flames, lightning struck the fearful trees on a November night. I was jogging with my dog down a beaten track with a howling wind trying to blow me off my feet. Suddenly, a mysterious voice screamed out, 'Help!'

I sprinted towards the ear-splitting screech, a house flickered in and out of view as I ran through the trees. I broke through into the clearing, it looked like a meteorite had marked the surface forever. I crept cautiously forward and saw a recorder in the middle of the clearing, it was playing eerie screams. Then everything went dark...

Matthew Knight (14)
Upper Wharfedale School, Skipton

Untitled

Evan walked down the ancient hallway, he was lost in the inky darkness of the house. Suddenly, he heard footsteps moving rapidly in front of him then they stopped.

'Hello?' he said. 'Hello?'

There was no answer. He walked forward then heard a low growl, then something running towards him. He started to run but it was getting closer and closer. He found a door and struggled to close it. He could hear something clawing against it. He backed away and he felt cold hands grabbing him. He broke free and kept running through the house, trying to escape quickly.

Patrick Weaver (14)
Upper Wharfedale School, Skipton

Unknown Streets

Pacing through the gloomy London streets, I feel a pair of dagger-like eyes stalk me, walking towards the light, a house glows, showing it's safe. The house beckons me in, almost inviting me. Approaching the house, I try the door to find it's locked, noticing a window, I climb through. On entering, a dead silence awaits. I continue heading up the stairs, pictures stare at me. Opening a door, I see people asleep, I know one thing which my mind screams at me. Carefully, I reached for my sharpened knife creeping towards them, with one action I...

Ben Evans (15)
Upper Wharfedale School, Skipton

It's Your Turn

There I was in what seemed like a peaceful forest. As the mist crept in, I began to remember what my friend had told me that there was once rumours of robotic bears that killed a little boy on this very spot. All evidence pointed to it, but the police still denied it. It was as if I could feel his paw on my back patting as if he wanted me to turn, so I did. There he was, robotic teeth glaring. His head tilted, shaking to the side, showing his wires. He said, 'It's your turn.'

Shana Longthorne (12)
Upper Wharfedale School, Skipton

The Woman In White

I walked through the empty field. I saw something, it looked like a woman in a white lace dress. Lily tripped over a gravestone, which pulled me away from my thoughts. I ran to help her up. Laughing, we walked to the pond, as she rubbed her sore leg. As I looked down into the water, I saw the reflection of a woman. Intrigued, I touched the water, which caused a light ripple. I turned away to face Lily. Suddenly, I was pulled into the water. All I saw was a woman screaming in my face...

Fizzah Shiaz (12)
Upper Wharfedale School, Skipton

Neglect

He'd managed to polish off a whole 18" pizza. It wasn't out of character, but it still titillated him, how he could consume so much with so little effort, regardless of the fact it had an abnormal taste. Afterwards, he tossed the pizza box to the floor, rolled over (which took him considerable effort) and drifted into slumber. In his gluttonous outburst, he neglected inspecting what he'd eaten. Not only did he eat something out of the norm, it was also now in him. Growing. Not that it mattered anyway, he'd never needed an excuse to be eating for two.

Michael Shann (17)
Wilberforce College, Hull

Est.1991

YOUNG WRITERS
INFORMATION

We hope you have enjoyed reading this book – and that you will continue to in the coming years.

If you're a young writer who enjoys reading and creative writing, or the parent of an enthusiastic poet or story writer, do visit our website www.youngwriters.co.uk. Here you will find free competitions, workshops and games, as well as recommended reads, a poetry glossary and our blog.

If you would like to order further copies of this book, or any of our other titles, then please give us a call or visit **www.youngwriters.co.uk.**

Young Writers
Remus House
Coltsfoot Drive
Peterborough
PE2 9BF
(01733) 890066 / 898110
info@youngwriters.co.uk